The
Cherokee Kid

David E. Tienter

THE CHEROKEE KID
By
David E. Tienter
Copyright
David E. Tienter 2016
Edited by Jennifer Zipperer
Cover by DataDesign
Cover Image: Dreamtime: PhilcoLD

Names, characters and incidents in this book are products of the author's imagination, or are used fictitiously. Any resemblance to actual events, locales, organizations, or persons, living or dead is entirely coincidental and beyond the intent of the author or the publisher.

ISBN: 1530483891
ISBN 13: 9781530483891

For Eric 1968 to 2015

The Cherokee Kid

THE WEAK MORNING sun was throwing a faint pink light over the small hidden campsite when Pinkney, ever true to his Indian heritage, rose and walked the outer perimeter of the camp. His eyes could pick up no movement anywhere; he'd crouched at the northern edge and listened carefully. No creak of saddle or faint sounds of men talking or horse hooves reached his ears. He was ready to do battle if attacked by the posse. No rope would end his life. He had little fear of death in battle, but the dread of years locked in a cage or quietly waiting to be a rope was a terror he would not face while still armed. Bringing in and saddling his horse, he felt prepared; ready to ride was never a bad thing. They would be coming. Like a wild wolf he could feel someone on his trail, and they would come shooting. It was hard to guess how close the posse could be, but he would be ready to move. After checking the loads in his pistols and stirring the ashes, he was able to resurrect a small fire and soon had coffee boiling. He put his few remaining hard tack biscuits in a pan with several chunks of bacon. He kicked Jaffee's boots as he walked past the sleeping mound of blankets. Jaffee was the last of the Wallace gang.

"Let's go, Jaffee. We gotta ride."

""Fuck off, half-breed, no black man tells me to get up."

Pinkney looked at the shape of the sleeping outlaw for a minute. Sighing slowly, he swallowed the bitter knowledge that this was his own fault. He never should have joined this band of down-at-the-heels southern boys. Their head man, Wallace, had needed another shooter for a herd of buffalo they had found out on the plains east of the hills. He and Wallace, being the better shots had done the killing, while the other three men skinned the brutes out. It was hot dirty work, but The Kid was short on money, and he figured to make a hundred for the week's work. He'd been double crossed while out scouting, the back-stabbing bastards had ridden off with the hides. On his return to camp, he was fuming, but it was already too dark to follow. Spending the night with a growing fury, he counted the hours until he could follow them.

In Belle Fourche, they had quickly sold the hides for a cut-rate price, meaning to ride before Pinkney, better known as The Cherokee Kid, could find them. Caution and sense had little meaning to the members of the gang, now with hot cash in their pockets they could not resist the open bar just down the street from where they stood. If the half-breed followed them, they would shoot him down. The gang was confident in their numbers and in Wallace's reputed speed with his sidearms. Before they left the bar, new plans had taken shape. Locals in the bar had complained about their part-time lazy sheriff, tasty news to hungry ears. The temptation of a fat bank in a small town with only amateur law was more than they could resist. This would be easy money.

The fast formed plan had Wallace going in first, followed by Verne, a fair gunhand, while Chandler held the horses and Jaffee stood watch outside. When the bank opened at ten, they were set. Things went south quick. The bank guard, proud of his job, turned out to be a stiff-necked, dedicated man. When he saw Wallace enter the bank with his gun in hand, he cocked the shotgun. Wallace's first bullet had hit the man, but the guard, tough as sun-dried leather, returned fire, killing Wallace just before he also died. The commotion brought the town's men running, and Jaffee began shooting at the men on the street. Verne staggered from the bank. Jaffe helped him get on his horse. A well-aimed rifle round caught Verne in the back throwing him forward in the saddle. Chandler caught a round while he was mounting his horse and he stayed on by gripping the saddle horn. The Kid's bad luck was that he had ridden into town minutes before, and now was dismounted and talking to the man at the livery stable, just as the outlaws were desperately trying to get out of town. Jaffee had seen him and cried to him for help. The man with a star on his vest shouted, "He's one of them," and began firing at The Kid. Caught in a situation with no good outcome, he'd run for his life. Both wounded men had died during the ride. Only Pinkney and Jaffee had escaped injury. With a posse hard on their trail, Pinkney led them through hard rocky canyons and over hill trails covered with deep pine needles, until late into the night. Exhausted, they set up a small camp deep under a sheltering butte, after not seeing the posse for several hours. Jaffee believed the star-led bunch had returned to Belle Fourche, giving up the pursuit. Pinkney was still angry that Jaffee had been one of those who had tried to rob his buffalo money, now he'd pulled Dan into the bank robbery also. Jaffee was not only slowing him down, but his attitude was irritating Pinkney even more.

"No sense in letting this lazy dolt get me hung," he thought.

Pinkney walked back to his pack, pulled out his .44 caliber buffalo rifle, walked back to where the man still lay, kicked him in the foot again. Then he put a round in the chamber. The loud mechanical click as the two inch long bullet shot home had Jaffee sitting tall, fully awake.

The Kid asked, "You know my name, Jaffee?

"Why you got yer buff banger out?"

"I asked you a question, Jaffee, you stupid piece of cow-flop."

"You're a, you're Dan Pinkney, they call you The Cherokee Kid."

"That would be Sir Daniel Pinkney to you. I was willing to drag your worthless butt around until I knew you only see my color. Stand up."

Jaffe stood slowly, watching the buffalo gun.

"Give me my money for the work on those buffalo hides."

"I've only got one hundred left," said Jaffee.

"Take it out of your pocket and drop it on the ground where you stand."

Jaffe pulled the loose bills from his pockets. "That's all I got."

"You tried to steal my share, then you pulled me into your holdup of that bank. I got every right to drill you where you stand. Still being a righteous black man, I'm going to give you a chance. I will count to ten, then I'm shooting."

"What about my horse and gear?"

"Totally up to you. You want to waste time on them, just make you an easier target for me. One," said The Kid.

Jaffee lit out for the east at a hard run.

Dan sat, ate breakfast, enjoyed his coffee, then loaded Jaffee's gear on the now extra horse and rode off, heading the horses off toward Deadwood. He calculated it was less than twenty miles away. He was short of rations, time to get some supplies. The posse or Earp would probably see Jaffee's trail, giving him extra time to get away.

Two hours later, he rode into Deadwood. The hair on his neck told him both Earp and the posse were following him, he dropped his order at the General Store and headed for the saloon. The heavy smell of pine boards, stale smoke, and the raw smell of spilled whiskey dominated the room. This early, only one other man was standing at the bar. He had a bottle, still half full, and a glass, now empty, in front of him.

Pinkney walked to the bar and shouted for the bartender.

"Here," said the lone drinker, "have a glass of mine. Jake's out back somewhere."

Pinkney reached over the bar, snagged two shot glasses off the shelf, walked over to the man. He filled both glasses, pushed one politely to the man, held the other glass high in a salute and gulped it down. "Thank you very much, sir, very generous of you."

The man at the bar looked casually at the short man with his face half covered by a beaten wide brimmed hat. He wore high-cuffed, dusty boots with well-rounded heels, worn out brown canvas britches held high by leather suspenders, a ratty, thin wool coat still buttoned, that covered a chambray shirt worn through at the collar. When he removed his hat, he revealed a sun- darkened face covered by skin stretched too tight. A heavy cropped moustache covered his upper lip and his eyes were deep seated with a flashy shine that saw much but showed little. He had an Indian countenance. The man was caked with sweat and smelled like horse urine. A bright red bandanna wrapped around his neck was the one unique thing he wore to set himself off. The man wore two .45 caliber pistols around his waist with the butts facing each other at belt buckle height. He removed the gloves from his hands revealing soft, non-calloused skin, not used for heavy work. He cared for his hands and kept them sensitive, ready for use.

Pinkney surveyed the man at the bar. He was dapperly dressed in a light brown suit, white shirt, new derby hat, and new boots.

The man said, "Only man I've heard of wears his guns that way is The Cherokee Kid. You must be Dan Pinkney. Wyatt left here an hour ago, hot to pick up your trail. You been running his ass off for the last two weeks. His poor mount's shoes are worn thinner than a dime."

"You a friend of Earp?" Pinkney had turned to face the dapper man. His hand lowered to his waist. His eyes aimed a hard threatening glance.

"I do claim that honor, sir. However I am not a lawman. Still, with five hundred on your head, I understand why you are a little suspicious. I would not spend too much time in town. You never know when one of these yahoos will be foolish enough to try to collect."

'You thinking about it?" Pinkney was still facing him, hand near his gun.

The man turned to look at the short, hazel nut colored man. Pinkney was fully braced against him as if daring him to try anything. "Before you pull that hog-leg, you might want to know that my name is John Henry Holliday. Some people call me Doc. It was the very dogs of hell that forced me into being a gunfighter, and I should probably tell you that I have never backed away from one. If you have heard of me, you know I would never kill a man for money. I am a gentleman, and I suggest you also act the part. Have another drink and part with me as a friend should."

Pinkney's face blanched slightly when he heard Doc's name. Nothing like bracing against the most notorious killer in the west. "Well sir, proud to meet you. Thank you for the whiskey. Hope we can remain friends. This is news for Earp. If you see him soon, there is a posse from Belle Fourche chasing me now also." He turned and left the bar. Doc listened for a few minutes, heard no shooting, turned to the bar, and began laughing. "You, Mr. Cherokee Kid, are a character cut as large as Wild Bill himself."

The Posse

ERNEST STEEL, THE sheriff, stopped the posse early on the first night while there was still enough light to set up camp. The long day began for him before dawn restocking his general store before opening.   His appointment as sheriff was never meant to be full-time work. He'd taken the job for the extra thirty bucks a month, together with the promise from the city council that his job would consist mostly of locking up drunks and delivering warrants. Nothing had ever been said of bank robberies or chasing fugitives all day with a patch-work posse, and yet here he was. His life had been behind a counter; selling, then restocking, and selling again.

Most of the men in the posse were familiar with spending nights out in the open. Sheriff Steel knew little about life outside Belle Fourche. He watched his men as they prepared for the night, assessing each man's capabilities. They had first set up a lariat corral. There had been few men in town at the time of the robbery and he had felt lucky to get seven men to join him in the chase. The two older men, Sam Winters and Cal McGregor, were having difficulty with the long ride. They owned ranches near Belle Fourche and had been in town for supplies. Both were important men in the small town and had been instrumental in getting him appointed sheriff. The hard day's ride showed in their faces. Clearly both were more worried about their spread than catching the outlaws.

Four of the men were cowboys. Steel had seen them around town, but knew little about them. They had been waiting in the Dog Ear Saloon to help Winters and McGregor with the supplies. Steel felt certain that all had ridden on the posse because their bosses expected it of them and, of course, there was a chance of financial gain with the reward on the outlaw's head. None of the cowboys were tired after the day of pursuit as they had spent much of their lives working from a saddle. They were the ones who started the campfire and prepared the site for the night.

The eighth man, Jake Andly, ran a small spread with his brother, just east of town. He worked for the sheriff occasionally as a deputy.

After everyone had slapped most of the trail dust from their clothes and eaten, they were still standing around the fire while several were making a smoke, when Cal McGregor spoke up. "We didn't catch him Ernie, chased his sorry ass through the heat and dust all day for nothing. Now what I want to know is, how far you plan on following his trail?"

"Until we have him tied to his horse or slung over it. Then we will take him back to Belle Fourche to bury him, or we'll hang him first, then bury him."

"You seem damn sure of yourself for a man who spent all day chasing the wind. What makes you think he's going to slow down for you? The way I see it, we chased him out of our country. He won't be coming back to rob our bank again. Time to go home. Someone else can deal with that little weasel."

There was a general rumble of agreement.

"When'd you get so old, Cal? I remember the day you'd have followed a cattle rustler for a week, to hang him for branding one of your calves."

"Them days is long in my past, Ernie. I'm heading back in the morning."

"Winters, you with me or you giving up too?"

"I'll be riding back with Cal. Wish you the best, but I'm too old for this crap."

"So we're down to six. I deputized you cowboys this morning and promised you a share of the reward. You knew what you were in for. Now who is still with me and who ain't got the sand to go on?"

Dratcher, one of the cowboys, spoke up. "We knew what we were signing on for, Sheriff. You promised us two dollars a day, a share of the reward and found, but can you promise us we'll still have jobs when we get back? We'll ride with our bosses and keep working. Something else to be thinking is that The Kid is riding into hostile territory. We follow him in there, we're going to have to battle Indians before we can even get to Pinkney. Half of us probably will be dead before we get back. There is also The Kid himself. He's as slippery as greased owl manure. Unless his horse gives out, we'll be chasing him in circles for weeks and still probably not catch him. Riding with you don't make good sense to us."

Sam Winters spoke up, "My men will have their jobs waiting for them if they choose to ride with you."

The sheriff looked at his crew sitting around the fire, drinking coffee, and passing a bottle one of the cowboys had brought. Only Jake was looking back at him. He knew there was little he could say. These were his townsmen. Cal and Sam were friends, but now when they pulled back in the morning, the cowboys would be riding back with them.

"Ain't like you didn't know what you signed on for. What'd you think, that we'd chase him a little while and he'd come running in with his hands held up? How easy did you think it would be to get a $500 reward? Well, any of you going on with me?"

Winters' hands had talked between themselves. "We will travel with you for another week, Sheriff. After that we're coming back."

"I'm still with you, Sheriff," said Jake. He was a tall, thin man, wearing worn, scruffy clothes and of them all, kept his own council.

When the sheriff had used him as a part-time deputy, he had found him to be reliable and a trustworthy backup. Sheriff Steel was a little disappointed that the two cowboys and Jake had agreed to continue on. At the time of the robbery, he'd seen The Kid ride in and knew there was a bounty on his head. Steel had shouted Pinkney was part of the robbery. He could certainly use the extra money to clear off some bills. If the others had all turned back, the sheriff would have the whole reward.

In the dim light of dawn, they collected the extra rations and ammo from the ranchers heading back to Belle Fourche and traveled south on The Kid's trail. The smaller posse rode faster now. At the outlaws' former campsite, they stopped and made breakfast. They picked up Jaffee's trail fast and the cowboys followed it less than five miles before capturing him. Jaffee was screaming about being forced to the bank by The Kid. Steel sent Winters' cowboys back to Belle Fourche with the prisoner, leaving the two lawmen to pursue The Cherokee Kid by themselves. Andly and Steel stood looking out across the prairie as they drank their coffee.

"This is my plan," he said to Jake. "The Kid will be moving slow, saving his mount. We'll both ride hard to get ahead of him. I want you to ride southwest for two hours, while I ride to the southeast. Then we'll both head straight south for several more hours. Ride hard, but keep your eyes peeled for a sign. At one o'clock, slow down and head back southeast. I will be doing the same and will plan on meeting you somewhere around dark. If you find him, don't try to take him alone, signal me with two rifle shots in the morning and we'll close in together. Somewhere along the path, we'll surely find some sign. He will be less careful now that he believes he's safe."

Jake headed his horse southwest and cantered away at a fast pace.

Chasing The Kid

LEAVING DEADWOOD, THE Kid traveled south through the last canyons and peaks of the Black Hills and into the uncharted lands of the wild territories. He knew the posse would hesitate before following him into the land still held by the hostile Sioux, Kiowa, and Ute Indian nations. He was still familiar with it to a degree since he had ridden through it years before. His life would end in agony if captured by the Kiowas or Utes, but he had spent enough time with the Arikara Sioux in South Dakota that he might be able to parlay passage if captured by them.

He kept his mount moving at a fast pace since he could switch off during the day with Jaffee's horse. He had to avoid exhausting them, but believed with the tandem pair he could easily outdistance the posse. The second day south of the hills, on the flat prairie, he ran across a set of tracks left by a single horse, late in the afternoon. He left the trail immediately, riding east at a brisk canter. Too many enemies were around him and the high bounty on his head was a continuing threat. 'Dead or Alive', the posters read, encouraging bounty hunters with no scruples to pursue him, and a black half-breed tends to stand out in the general population.

Several hours off the trail where he had seen the tracks, after riding through the prairie grasses and across what rocky outcroppings he came across, he stopped while the sun still displayed its dying beauty against the evening sky. He set up his camp in a dry creek arroyo with a small, hot fire to heat his coffee and evening meal. He unsaddled his horses, then hobbled them to let them graze on what fodder they could find. His biscuits and bacon eaten, a hot cup of coffee by his side, he relaxed against his saddle and lit one of the cigars he had purchased in Deadwood.

The cool quiet of the evening, accompanied by a coyote serenade, began to drain the tension out of him. The horses, ever vigilant, would let him know if intruders were around. Pulling his bedding up, he soon drowsed off to sleep.

Deep into sleep, his unconscious mind heard the slight unrest of the horses and he immediately became fully awake. He stood, looking hard into the starlit night, but could see nothing. Abruptly, a match lit up the night as though someone was lighting a smoke. Dan picked up his rifle and moved several yards back from the campsite where no flicker of firelight would expose him.

"Hallo the camp," he heard. "I'm riding north to the Black Hills and smelled your campfire. Figured you might enjoy a little company this beautiful evening."

"You alone?" asked The Kid.

"Yep. Traveling light, figured I could get to the gold fields before all the good sites were taken."

"Come on in then," said The Kid, throwing a few dried sticks on the still smoldering campfire. "Better to have an enemy close than having him watch you through the night," he thought, "Too easy to set up an ambush at first light."

A lone horseman approached. Sitting on his horse, the man looked down at The Kid, who was still holding his rifle in his right hand with the barrel pointed at the ground.

"Your coffee smells heavenly. Ran out of it myself two days ago."

"Help yourself," said The Kid, pointing at the boiling pot.

The man dismounted and pulled a cup from an overloaded saddlebag. Dan could see a rock hammer and a sluice pan tied to the pack. The man crouched by the fire and filled his cup.

"Thanks, neighbor. Been a long ride up from Dodge and I could feel hostile eyes on me most of the way."

"Another two days and you'll be out of this flat prairie and into the Black Hills. Just came from there myself."

"Damn good news. Gold just laying around there to be picked up, like they say?"

"Never bothered looking," said The Kid.

The man stood, walked around the campfire, and extended his right hand to Dan.

"My name is Jake Slags," he said, "and you'll hear of me again, cause I'm going to find enough gold to buy St. Louie."

Dan ignored his hand. "I'm Dan the Gambler. But I don't gamble with strangers in the night." He lifted his rifle until it was pointed at the man. "I want you to unhook that gunbelt and toss it over by my saddle. Then get your rifle and put it over there too. That way, they will be handy if we need them and we will both be able to get some rest tonight."

"That seems damn unfriendly. You trying to rob me, I only got maybe twenty dollars to my name."

"Do as I say," Dan said, "and you'll be alive with your twenty dollars in the morning."

The man slowly undid his belt, tossed his sidearm over toward Dan's saddle, then went to his horse and brought back the rifle which he also laid by Dan's bedroll.

"Thank you," said Dan. "Now take care of your mount, bring your gear in, and we can be friendly before we sleep."

Jake shuffled around, performed his chores, fried up some bacon on the fire, and finally sat down across the fire from Dan.

"I hope all your plans work out up there in the gold fields."

"Where you headed now, gambling man?"

"To the very center of gambling in the west: the end of the line, Dodge City. It's time I took life a little easy. Maybe I can get used to city living."

"Well, Dodge is getting to be pretty big now, what with the cattle and cowboys crowding in every day. Them cowboys got some fat pockets after getting paid. I was only there a couple of days, but I sure got tired of them drunk yahoos shooting up the sky most of the night."

"Sounds perfect to me," said Dan as he pulled his blankets back up. "See you again at sunrise."

Back On The Trail

AT FIRST LIGHT, Jake slowly opened one eye to look at Dan. He wanted the reward that would come from capturing The Cherokee Kid. Extra money would help with needed repairs on his spread, but the campsite was empty.

"Damn," said Jake, standing up. His guns were still where The Kid had left them. He picked up his rifle and went looking for his horse. No horse in sight, but he did find the cut hobbles lying in the dirt. "Double damn." His hopes to be the man who brought in The Cherokee Kid had scattered on the morning air. He jacked a shell into his rifle and fired twice into the air. An hour later, the sheriff came riding into the campsite.

"Found him last night, but he got the drop on me. He was gone before daybreak, cutting the hobbles on my horse. He is a shifty little devil."

"Let's have some coffee, then you can take my horse for a look-see. Maybe you can find that knot headed mount of yours," said the sheriff.

The horse rounded up, sitting across the fire from each other, the sheriff asked, "Where did you get the sluice pan and rock hammer?"

"Found a bunch of scattered bones during the ride, figured if I ran into Pinkney, I would use them for an excuse to be riding north."

"Good thinking", said the sheriff. "What's the chances he bought your story?"

"Doubt it. I think he saw right through me. Man on the run don't trust no one much."

"Any ideas on which way he went?"

"Been cogitating on that all morning," said Jake. "He told me he was a gambler headed for Dodge City. Said since that was the end of the line, cowboys would be crowding the table to give their money away to a good gambler. Everyone west of St. Louie knows Selina is the end of the line. One sure thing is that he isn't headed south. I'm sure he won't head back north, too many people looking for him there. No reason to go east that I can think of. Gotta be headed west to California or maybe Oregon. Somewhere he can fit in with people and not stand out."

"I think you're dead on. But let's track him a ways just to see what he does. Shouldn't be too difficult to track two horses in this grass."

Wyatt Steps In

DAN LEFT THE camp in early dark, riding straight south. He passed a large outcropping of rock as the light from a dappled sky began to give form to the prairie. He continued straight south until he came to a small creek, giving his horses plenty of time to drink, backtracked his trail to the rocky outcropping, then dismounting, he led the animals over the rocks, brushing away any stray tracks with the foliage from a sage brush plant. At the far edge of the rocks, he remounted and pointed the head of his cayuse straight west.

Deepening purple twilight forced him to an early camp setup. He had ridden easy, sparing undo strain on his mount. A quick meal, hobbled horses off grazing, within minutes he was dozing off.

The metallic click of a rifle chambering a round sounded as loud as a dry lightning bolt in the stillness of the night. Dan came fully awake, sitting upright in the dark, he reached for weapons, finding that they were not where he'd left them.

"My rifle is aimed at your heart," said a gravelly voice from a figure slightly outlined by the starlight. "Try not to do something stupid, cause I can bring you back dead, no questions asked."

The dark man threw dry kindling on the smoldering coals of the campfire. By the soaring flames, Dan saw the man clearly. A walrus bar moustache crowded his face. He wore a long black coat and there was a star on his chest. His rifle was centered on Dan.

"Evening, Earp," said Dan, raising his hands to show they were empty.

"Put your hands down, Kid. I'm here to talk. Might have to take you back, but lets us talk a little first. The warrant I have is for the man you killed in Deadwood. Tell me what happened. Tell it straight."

"Give me a minute to get the coffee on then, and I'll tell you 'bout that killing."

Coffee in one hand, smoke held in the other, Dan began his story. "I's heading out of Deadwood, heard a big row on the corner ahead of me and it got my attention. Bunch of locals was gathered, cheering and a hollering. Still mounted, I could see over the sorry lot. The center of the commotion was a big dirty man, took him to be a mule skinner. He was making his bullwhip snap and crackle. I could see he was beating a smallish man huddled against the wall for cover. A little closer and I could see it was just a kid. The skinner was shouting, he didn't like thieving Injun low lives, skulking around and stealing his stuff.

"The kid wasn't fighting back, he had no defense at all, just huddled in the street, covered with blood, while the man kept on beating him. The rabble scum around him were cheering him on. I put my spurs to my mount and he charged through the crowd, smashing head-on into the skinner knocking him backwards and to the ground. I got off my horse to help the kid up, heard the man behind me stand up and call me another low life Injun breed. I expected to feel that lash, instead, he tried to draw his gun. I could see he's primed up on bottle courage and the cheers of the people. Had a feeling he was going to draw, would have dissuaded him if I could a, but he was well past reason. Put three rounds into his chest. He must have been very strong cause that .45 didn't knock him over. He just sat down, leaned forward, and slid into the dust. Helped the kid up on my horse and the two of us rode him back to his mother's house. Not apologizing for it either, even if you going to hang me. That skinner would have beaten him to death, cheered on by that bar scum hanging around."

"From what I've learned about it already, I suspect you're right. Talked to the kid's mother, she backs up your story. Trouble I got is that warrant to take you back. Even if you're innocent, you'll still get convicted and hung. The closed minded son-of-a-bitches don't much like blacks and they hate Indians. They'd find you guilty just on general purposes. So I ain't taking you back. I'll be judge and jury in this: I pronounce you innocent. But I would advise you not to return to Deadwood. Sounds to me like you should have killed a few more of them," said Earp.

"Heard you robbed a bank in Belle Fourche. I don't have that warrant, so not my business. Best watch out for a posse."

"How'd you ever find me out here?" asked Dan.

"Purely it was just blind luck. I tell you right now, Kid, I'm tired of wearing a badge. This lawman crap is getting old. Too much time chasing innocent men who end up getting hung anyways. Lately the whole west seems rope happy. On my way to Dodge right now, and stumbled across you in the dark. Thinking I might open a bar in Dodge." Earp turned and walked into the dark, Dan heard the sound of his horse in the dark.

Hostile Ute's

THE CAMP BEGAN to lighten to a dark gray long before the sun bridged the east. The Kid made coffee before bringing his horses in. Unknown to him was the determination of the posse. They could have traveled late and now could have closed on him. He rode straight west. The seemingly empty prairie stretched out as far as he could see.

He had saddled Jaffee's horse this morning, thinking it would be the fresher mount. He wasn't overly surprised when by noon, under the relentless sun the mount began to tire. Changing the saddles and gear, he continued heading west on his animal, moving at a fast gait. That worthless Jaffee hadn't even been able to pick out a good horse.

This prairie can't go on forever, he thought. Somewhere out here there has to be water. No water for the animals would have them in worse shape by tomorrow. Still, his course was set and the truth was obvious, going either north or south would be just as bad.

Near late afternoon, he dismounted and walked the horses for a while. He had to work the stiffness out of his back and legs. In the distance, he saw a cloud of dust approaching him rapidly. Too late to flee, he swung his horse sideways and standing behind it, drew his buffalo gun out and cocked it.

Seven Indians pulled to a halt thirty yards in front of him. He didn't recognize the tribe, so he raised his right hand as a gesture of good will, and called out a greeting in Cherokee. One of the Indians called back in English.

"I am Standing Tall of the Utes," The Kid heard in response.

The greeting raised his hopes. Seven men, several with rifles, faced him. He could kill one, but down to his colts, they would stand off a ways and kill him. If they would parley, he might still get out of this with his hair.

"I am Pinkney of the Cherokees. My father was the great Chief Wounded Elk."

"Why are you here on our lands, Pinkney?"

"I seek passage to the west. I have brought a horse to give as tribute to the Utes if they will allow me passage."

"Why do you hold your rifle aimed at us?"

"This is a hard country. Many enemies search for me. I need to find out if you are friends and willing to trade."

"Put down your rifle and I will approach."

The Kid lowered his rifle and leading Jaffee's horse forward, met the Indian leader halfway.

"You do appear to be half Indian."

"My mother was a slave woman for the Cherokees. My father freed her before I was born. I am from the land of Oklahoma."

Looking over Jaffee's horse carefully, the Indian said, "I, Standing Tall, accept your tribute and will allow you passage to the west."

"Also, my friend," said Pinkney, "would you tell me how far to water?"

"Before dark you will cross a creek, running water is always best. Many alkali ponds are near. Do not take water from them."

The Utes took the horse and rode off with the other braves.

The Kid walked back to his horse, stood quietly several minutes while he rolled a smoke. His legs had begun to tremble. Fortunately the fear hadn't affected him when he was before the Indians, or they might have killed him. Bravery was highly prized by all Indians and one brave man facing off against seven impressed them enough to let him go. If he had shown fear, they would have two horses now, and a scalp hanging from the leader's horse.

By dark, Dan was camped by the river while his horse rested and fed on the lush grasses near the water.

Riding west with a much fresher mount, he could see the dark purple of the mountains ahead of him. His spirits rose, and soon he was traveling easier. Three more days and he entered the foothills of the Big Horns. The peace of the forest was soothing to him. He camped two nights at his first site with water for the pony and grass for it to eat. He slept soundly, while maintaining a watch during the day. No sign of the posse.

On the third day, he left the campsite at full alert. The Kid had seen riders on the prairie. They appeared to be cowboys riding herd, but to a man running from a posse, riders meant danger. Heading straight up the foothill, he stopped and shaking his feet out of the stirrups, slid off the horse.

His senses on high alert now, he could hear the sounds of men in the next valley. Ten feet below the ridgeline, Dan lashed the horse to low hanging branches, and crawled up the ridgeline to look into the next valley. It was v-shaped, opening to the prairie on the east and lined with mountains on the west.

A small cabin was located six hundred yards to the west of where The Kid lay watching. There was a large corral built with a lean-to inside it to provide shade for the horses it contained. Most of the animals were crowded together, pushing to get into the shade. A small scurry of chickens scratched and pecked at the bare ground surrounding the buildings. A yellow mix-breed dog lay in the shade, and watched the hen with chicks hungrily. There was no sign of the posse or other men.

Dan watched a bonneted woman in a homespun, brown dress chop firewood near the homestead cabin. He had heard the sounds of her splitting wood. Two younger children sat quietly on the porch, playing a game with sticks and rocks on the front porch. Calculating rapidly, Dan figured he had a good two day jump on the posse. Experience told him there were no men at the homestead or the woman would not be doing the hard labor.

There were several horses in the corral, maybe he could trade up his tired mount for a fresher one. Although his funds were running low, now dipped to only ninety dollars, twenty or thirty bucks spent here could help him immensely. The deciding factor, in approaching the homestead, was his sympathy for the woman doing the onerous task of wood splitting. He had watched his mother work herself to death as a freed slave on the Cherokee Trail of Tears, performing such tasks when he was but a child. Finally, with his mind set, he remounted and descended into the valley.

He approached the house slowly, and began hailing it well before he rode in. The dog ran out and barked threateningly, then retreated to the safety of the cabin. The woman surprised, turned to look at him, then called to her children, and picked up her rifle. They all went into the cabin. He could hear the slide and thunk as the bolt was thrown on the door.

He uncinched his mount, threw the saddle and blanket over the stout wood fence enclosing the corral. Drawing a bucket of water from the well, he let the horse drink its fill before turning it loose in the corral.

Pinkney surveyed the layout close-up. The cabin appeared well built and able to withstand the winter storms that would blast down off the mountain. There were well positioned gun ports he could see. A rifle was pointed out the front port at him now, but he ignored it. The corral and lean-to looked solid and well built. A well had been dug close to the water trough for the horses, and the dirt removed had been packed up to the edge, about two feet high. It looked to Dan that well safety was not a high priority by the person who dug it, but the homesteader appeared to take good care of his equine stock.

A supply of ten to fifteen felled trees was located on the west side of the house. The logs looked to be placed so as to provide cover if the homestead was attacked from the west. A small vegetable garden was marked off by string tied to sticks, south of the well.

Removing his jacket, and laying his pistols and gun belt on the porch, he picked up the axe, and began splitting the wood already cut into short sections. He split and stacked enough to complete a good two week supply. He assumed the woman was married, and it was reasonable to him that the missing husband would return within two weeks. He picked up one of the logs, balanced it on the wood stack and using the crosscut saw lying there, sawed one of the felled logs into two foot sections, in case the woman would need them later.

Covered with sweat and tired, he went to the well and drew a fresh bucket. The water was cool and tasted good. He washed himself down to his waist, and poured the remaining water in the horse trough. Noticing how low it was on water, he poured buckets of water in the trough. The horses began crowding around now that the water was at least nose deep and sucked down the water noisily. He refilled it when they had backed off a bit.

Then as a cool twilight breeze began to blow, he walked to the door of the cabin and knocked loudly.

"Ma'am, I would like to talk to you about trading that tired mount of mine for a couple of yours. I am unarmed and will back off into the yard so you can see me clearly."

He heard the door latch slide back.

"No need for that, mister," the woman said. "I've prepared a meal for you. Would you please come in to eat?"

A big smile swept across Dan's face, "That's the friendliest thing anyone has said to me in a month. I would be proud to eat with you."

He removed his hat and slowly entered the sparsely furnished cabin. At the center of the one room were a roughhewn table and four handmade stools, with a place set for only one. He sat before a heaping plate of hot porridge. The dog, a small mongrel, barked at him a few times. The little boy said, "Ruff, no, get to your corner." When Dan ignored the little dog, it went and lay down, watching Dan carefully.

"Sorry, but I only have water to offer you for a drink. My coffee supplies have been exhausted. My husband is in town now getting supplies." The woman stood to one side in front of the children. Her rifle was still close to her hand.

Hungry now after the long day, Dan sat and ate several large spoonfuls quickly before looking up to see the children watching him eat. He put one more spoonful into his mouth thoughtfully.

"Please excuse me for one minute," he said. Rising, he left the cabin, went to his saddle, and drew out what little stores of bacon he had left. He picked up his last two cans of peaches and what coffee still remained, and returned to the cabin. Laying the supplies on the table, he said, "A meal shared always tastes better. How about we cook up some of that meat, open them peaches, and share a steaming cup of coffee together?"

The woman looked at him with a stern frown. "No, thanks. We may be just scratching through the hard way, but we'll feed the kids ourselves. I appreciate the wood you cut for us, it's worth a meal. It don't make you a friend, and it surely doesn't make you trustworthy."

"Damn," thought Dan, "save me from these stiff necked proud people."

"Well, madam, tell you the truth, not much nourishes this old cowboy's heart than seeing them little tykes eating and enjoying themselves. And please call me Dan. My name is Dan Pinkney. I'd consider it a kindness if we could all sit together. If you wish to keep your rifle handy, I understand. Those kids look a little hungry though. I swear to you, I have never hurt a woman or a child."

Judging carefully what the man had said, and looking at the want in the children's eyes seeing the food, she put the rifle back on its wall rack. "Well," said the woman, "since you put it that way." She had the bacon cooking and the coffee brewing in another minute. Dan noticed the stern look began to leave her face as she worked around the cook stove.

"Well, Mr. Pinkney, I'm Mrs. Hilderbrant. The boy is named Adam and the girl is Jewel. My husband, Burt Hilderbrant, left to get supplies five days ago. He should be riding in tomorrow."

She divided Dan's porridge onto four plates, dressed it up with bacon, and poured the bacon drippings over the plates. Opening the peaches and dumping them into a bowl, she placed the bowl in the middle of the table. "Come children, come," she made welcoming motions with her hands to the children, "we will all eat together tonight."

Hesitantly, the two nervous children, with eyes opened wide in anticipation, took chairs at the table. They watched their mother eagerly and after she had bowed her head, they ate rapidly. Several minutes later, with the food consumed and peaches gone, Dan and Mrs. Hilderbrant sat at the quiet table with steaming cups of coffee.

Dan smiled at her, "That was a great meal. Thank you, but ma'am, could I trouble you for two more glasses?"

Mrs. Hilderbrant looked at him for a moment, then as if accepting something, rose and brought two clean glasses to the table.

"Now kids, I really like peaches," he said as he picked up the bowl in the middle of the table, "but what I like even better is sipping the liquid left over."

He poured the juice equally into the glasses and pushed them over to the children.

"Trying taking just a small sip at first," he said.

Adam completely ignored his advice and gulped it down in two big swallows. Jewel began taking small sips, savoring every second of the sweet treat until her glass was empty.

Their mother chased them both outside, "Get some playing done before bed. Adam, make sure Jewel stays away from the well."

Dan, coffee cup in hand, walked out into the cool breeze of the night. He sat on the edge of the porch and began constructing a smoke. Lighting it, he took a deep drag and relaxed, enjoying the children playing at their games. Several minutes later, the woman followed him out and stood behind him.

"Beautiful evening."

"It is all of that," said the woman. "The heat of these days can weigh on you. Nights like this keep you struggling on. It was wonderful of you to bring the food in for the kids. That was the first time they had ever eaten at a table with adults. You can tell they really enjoyed it, especially the peach juice."

"No trouble for me, and it was warming to watch them eat. Hope you have got enough for the little tykers to eat tomorrow?"

"My husband Burt should be back early with fresh supplies. We'll be just fine. It's too dark to trade horses now, could you return for that in the morning?"

"Well, madam, I'll bunk down over by the corral if that is acceptable to you. I've gotten sorta used to sleeping near that old cayuse of mine. If you'd prefer, I'll ride on a distance and bunk down later."

"You're welcome to sleep down by the corral, Dan. You must be a little weary from the work." In her heart she was hoping he'd be gone. If her husband showed up while he was here, he'd kill the man and beat her. He trusted no man and hated Mexicans, Indians, and Blacks equally.

Dan crushed his cigarette beneath his foot, handed his empty cup to the woman. "See you tomorrow then." He walked down to the corral, making a wide loop around the open well. "Thank you for the wonderful meal."

He could hear the children still chatting excitedly as their mom rounded them back into the house. His last thought before he slept was, "Waiting for supplies can be a long hungry time."

The Hunt

A FAINT MAUVE wash was beginning to push back the night when Dan felt small hands pushing at his legs. He'd awakened at the sound of the cabin door opening.

"You awake yet, mister?"

"Yep, you caught me just lying here with my eyes closed thinking."

"Whatcha thinking about, mister?"

"Thinking you ought to call me Dan to start with. Nother thing I's thinking is maybe I oughta ride up that hillside there a ways and shoot a big buck for breakfast. Whatcha think about that?"

"I's wondering if you's thinking about taking me along."

"Well Adam, I'm sure my horse can carry us both, but you gotta get your mom's permission before I take you. Otherwise she would worry about you too much."

He heard scurrying boots and a yapping dog heading for the cabin. Standing and stretching, Dan stomped his feet to get the blood pumping right, then pulled out a paper and began rolling an eye-opener.

"Mom said I could go iffen we wouldn't be gone too long. Cause otherwise, I might not be here when Dad comes back."

"Tell her I'll go as fast as I can, and that we are using one of the horses as a pack animal. No telling how long until we can find a deer though."

Dan saddled his horse, threw a rope around another stout looking pony, and got everything else ready for the hunt. As he rode past the cabin, Adam came sailing out. "I can go."

"Ever ride before?"

"Nope, but I learn fast."

"Stick up your left hand," Dan told him. He caught the child's arm, and swung him up behind him. "Just hold on to my belt and let me know if you're having any problems. The secret is relaxing so you can move with the rhythm of the horse." Ruff was running about the yard, obviously worried about Adam.

"Will he be okay, or you want me to put him in the house?"

"He'll probably run along. Don't worry, dogs are made for hunting."

Dan tied the packhorse to his saddle horn and walked slowly out of the yard; about a hundred yards down the trail he kicked the horse up to a slow trot. Adam rode well, staying tight as a tick. Soon he rode the horse at a natural gait up the hill and within an hour was far enough up into the bluffs to start looking for signs of deer. The early morning light had begun to burn off the morning mist deep in the forest, when Dan dismounted near the top of a ridge. He tied his horses to the stout lower branch of a tree, and then helped Adam down.

"Quiet now little man, we're going to be looking for a big buck in the next valley. Deer have keen hearing. They can hear a mouse move in a rainstorm and smell a man a hundred yards off."

Together the two crept up to the top of the ridge, lay belly down on the forest floor, and began searching the game path in the next valley for a big buck. Dan would take a doe if he had to, making sure the family would have something to eat. Still he would much prefer to bag a buck.

The early morning hour, excitement of going on his first ride and hunt, had a tired Adam's head nodding, and soon after settling into the surveillance, he began to sleep, with one arm over his dog for warmth.

The roar of the rifle startled him and he leaped to his feet, forgetting momentarily where he was. The dog was barking loudly, frightened by the sound of the gun.

"You okay, Adam?" asked Dan. "We just got our first buck together. There will be good eating for a few days."

"You really got one?"

"Yep. He's laying down there just a little east of that big maple. See that one with the gnarly knob on it? Yep, that's the one," he told Adam, when he pointed at it. "Come on, let's get the horses down there and dress this guy out."

Down near the slain deer, Dan built a small fire. He tied the deer's back legs to a low branch. It was just high enough for its head to clear the ground. He drew his knife from the sheath in his boot and cut its throat to let it bleed out. He cut the deer from its anus down to its neck. Pulling on the innards and cutting when needed, he removed the animal's insides. Digging around in the still steaming pile, he pulled out the heart and the liver. He carefully sliced four small pieces off each, and slowly fed them into the fire with his head bowed.

"Why do you do that?" asked Adam.

"Part of my heritage. We always honor the animal for giving his life, that we may survive. Many people eat meat without thinking of the animal that died so they could eat. It can be a hard thing to kill an animal and this is our way to show the animal that we appreciate his sacrifice."

Dan held the rest of the liver up to Adam. "Here, you want a bite of this?"

Adam looked at the raw bloody organ and hesitated. Dan took a large bite, chewed it with relish and again offered it to Adam. This time Adam took a small bite.

"Hey," he said, "that's great."

Dan gave the rest of the liver to the dog, who ate it greedily.

"Now let's get him packed down to your mom, so everyone will get something to eat for breakfast."

Back near the homestead, Dan saw that twenty to thirty head of cattle had moved in around the cabin. They were crowding against the corral to get at the water. Some had knocked down the rope around the garden and were feeding on the vegetables the woman had planted.

Dan stopped his horse to look over the homestead. He could not see any riders there, only the cattle. He dismounted, lifting Adam down. Unfastening the packhorse, he handed the rope to Adam.

"Wait till I come for you."

He rode down toward the cabin, followed by the barking mutt. Dan drew his revolver, and fired one shot. The dog didn't like the noise of the gun and barked louder. The cattle began moving away from them. His horse instinctively began to round them up into a single moving herd with Dan shouting at them, then he fired again, and they picked up speed.

Quickly he had the cattle moving rapidly down the valley, away from the homestead. Returning to Adam, he caught up the rope from the packhorse. Within minutes they were back at the cabin and were unloading the deer meat. He tied the venison to the edge of the roof on the northern slope of the cabin where it would be in shade most of the day. He was skinning the deer when Mrs. Hilderbrant turned the corner of the building. She was patting her hair down and brushing the front of her dress. "Glad you brought him back safe, sounds like he had a wonderful time, but this cabin can be quiet when he's not around. You two got a real beauty.

"Thanks," said Dan, "Adam and me were lucky alright. Big one walked right by where we were laying."

"Let's have breakfast before we talk. It will give the tykes a chance to wind down a little," said Dan, cutting off a long strip of tenderloin. "Try this section, I'm sure you'll love it."

"You're right, you're absolutely right. But I'm going to say one quick 'thank you' for chasing those cattle out of my garden. Give me twenty minutes and breakfast will be ready." She smiled at Dan before turning back to the cabin.

Dan walked down to the well, closely followed by Adam and Jewel. He drew a bucket of water and all three washed up. Dan poured the remaining water into the horse trough and the three headed back to the cabin. Dan did not like the children near the well, too dangerous. That would have to be taken care of soon.

The succulent odor of the frying meat filled the air and sharpened the hunger of those still outside; when the kids' mother called, they all headed for the door. She had the venison steaks cooked and coffee brewing. All four sat at the table and ate together.

"Sorry the coffee is a little weak. This is the last of what you brought in."

"It's weak but warm; tastes good to me. Shall we take it outside and look at the day?"

They stood on the porch watching the children play. "Not too close to the well, Adam."

"How long them ranchers been letting their cattle drift?"

"Almost since the first. My husband chased them off like you did. They's Slash S cattle. Man named Sweets owns the ranch. Mr. Hilderbrant was going to Sweet's ranch to talk to him on this trip. I hope when he returns with the supplies he will have good news."

"When he rides in, I'll be moving on. Meanwhile, I figured to do a few chores around the place, if that's okay with you. My hoss has been resting. I'm giving him another day or two, then he'll be ready to ride again. Sorry, but I won't need to trade."

After finishing his coffee and lingering over a smoke, Dan walked down to the lumber pile. He worked one log free and balanced it over the other logs leaving one end sticking out over ten feet. With the crosscut, he cut the length off, pulled the log up high enough to leave another ten foot section, and then cut that one off. Splitting both log sections down the middle, he hooked up a horse and dragged them down by the well. He dug a three foot deep hole on each side of the well. Working on one log, he cut out and smoothed a notch in the middle of the top of the log. An hour later, he had a drawing frame over the well. Riding back up into forest, he cut a score of fresh branches and dragged them back to the well. Working the fresh boughs around the buried logs, soon he had the well covered as best he could. He knew the branches would dry and have to be replaced, but for now the children would no longer worry so much about falling in, and the crossbeam over the top made it much easier to pull a full bucket up from the water. Surprising to Dan, the little dog and Adam had hung by his side all day.

The dog had been quiet, but Adam had been full of questions.

"Dan, Dan, why don't you wear your guns when you're working?"

"They get a little heavy and are in my way for chopping."

"But what if rustlers come?"

"Well, Ruff will let us know in time for me to get them."

"Going deer hunting again?"

"Maybe, but your dad should be here soon, then I'll probably have to move on."

"He needs a lot of help. You oughta stay and help him."

"We'll see. Most guys want to run their place themselves though."

"My dad doesn't ever wear guns."

"Guns aren't always the best thing to have around."

"Me and Jewel sure hope you stay around."

By the time he finished the well, the blue twilight sky had begun to blow a cool breeze against the hard land. Jewel came running to get Adam and him for supper.

The woman had found a little flour and cornmeal, mixed venison chunks into the doughy mixture, and fried it all up. It tasted great for an evening meal. The coffee was gone now, but after the hot day, water tasted great. For one more evening, Dan and the woman stood on the porch and watched the children play, no longer worrying that they would get too close to the well.

Lugunea Hilderbrant

HE HAD NOT noticed the motionless silent woman standing against the cabin wall watching him ride out. She felt her heart tear a little in her chest, knowing she would probably not see him again.

She knew a man like Dan was tied to nothing. He rode as only he wished. She had no power or right to hold him here. Burt could return at any time and he would kill Dan if he found him here. Still, the time without Burt had been as sweet as the time spent with Dan.

Looking back, her wedding day stood out foremost in her litany of horrible memories. It was early afternoon in the dreary one-dog town when Anne made her marriage vows.

The strange man across from her in the tiny church barely looked at her as they said, "I do." Her father and brothers had wakened her late in the night. She'd been told to shut up and get dressed. Tossed in a wagon, she'd been taken to the church.

Ten minutes of a bumpy, dusty ride, and she was standing before a drunken judge. Her wedding dress was the same dirty clothes she had worn all week. Now a complete stranger was standing next to her. Five minutes later, she was married. Neither her father nor brothers said a thing. They hurried out the door eager to spend the twenty-five dollars they had received for her. She was not sad to see them go and had never missed them.

Shiftless, lazy trash, they'd moved from one dirty town to another taking advantage of what they could rake off easy or steal that which wasn't guarded. She had been their cook-seamstress-cleaning girl with blows provided frequently if she was not fast enough. She prayed they were all dead.

At first, she had hopes that Burt would be better, a decent man. But he too was a grafter - cheating, stealing, and always moving to the next Promised Land, usually a few steps in front of the law.

Two years ago, he had discovered an ambushed wagon on the prairie near Dry Creek. The man and woman had been brutally slaughtered and their possessions scattered, but Burt dug through everything and searched the bodies. He had salvaged several dresses for her and a pair of boots for himself. He also found three hundred dollars' worth of gold in a pouch, under the man's body. He had used the money to buy the homestead. In the seven years of their marriage, he had probably spoken less than ten words to her. As far as she knew he had never bathed, or communicated in more than mono-syllabic grunts. She had washed his clothes, once, shortly after they were married. He was angry when presented with the clean clothes, and had been upset with her for several days. After that she had washed her own clothes and ignored his. She noticed that he returned from town wearing new jeans every few years. And once he had brought her back the rough dress she still wore. Her favorite times were when he would disappear for a week or two leaving her alone. She assumed he went to town, as he usually returned with supplies. He ate little but meat and beans and cornbread, but she had put in a small garden and raised a few vegetables. The seeds were hard to come by. She dried and stored them after harvest.

In her married life she retained all her former jobs, but now she was his brood cow too. Both children had been born without assistance for her. Pain and dirt and lots of blood were what she remembered of childbirth.

Why he had wanted children was a complete mystery to her. He seemed to hate them when he was not ignoring them. They couldn't talk to him, or sit at the table until he had finished eating. If they got in his way or made noise or just irritated him, he dealt with it by a blow or a kick, if not to them, to her. He ignored her except when meal time came around or if he needed help in foaling a mare.

"If there is a God out there, let that ugly bastard roast in hell with my father," was her usual prayer. Now she had also begun to pray that Dan Pinkney would return.

Meeting Slash S

IN THE COLD of the graying morning, Dan saddled his mount after packing all his gear. Wearing his jacket, he rode out of the homestead, heading south for the first half mile. Turning east, he kicked his horse up to an easy riding gait with the slowly breaking sun directly ahead of him and the looming black of the Big Horn Mountains to his rear. Several miles out from the cabin, he'd stopped his horse to check the loads, not wanting to handle the weapons in sight of the woman or her kids. Five hours later in the growing heat, he reached the brush lining the first of the fordings between the homestead and the town. Dismounting, he let his horse have a breather and drink his fill. Dan filled his canteens, always better to have too much water than too little.

The shallow, meandering creek he now crossed had been a churning mountain torrent fifteen miles back, but the flatness of the mesa not only split it into creeks, but slowed the water flow. Within another few miles, he figured it would be totally absorbed into the dryness of the plain. Dan understood now why a rancher was trying to drive the Hilderbrants off their site. The precious water was more plentiful closer to the foothills of the mountains and without plentiful water, cattle numbers would be limited.

An hour after the crossing, sprinkles of cows and calves began to cross his track, looking unhappy and moving restlessly. Soon, off to the right, he saw a chuck wagon with a group of eight cowboys seated around it. It was round up time and the cowboys were branding the calves birthed since last year.

Pinkney reined in and sat waiting, unsure of what reception he would receive. He remained in the saddle until the wagon boss called to him. "Might just as well get some coffee and grub. You're welcome to come on in, stranger."

Wagon boss Slocum had been a top hand in his youth. Several years back his horse had shied from a rattler and rolled onto his left leg. The bones and knee shattered, he had a stiff leg now and could no longer work on a horse. But the rancher, Mr. Sweets, had confidence in him and put him in charge of the chuck wagon. He could handle the job easily, and kept a stern hand over the two groups of cowboys he managed. He only brought in one gang of eight cowhands at a time so he could watch and listen to them better. He found out much sooner of any problems he might have to fix.

Dan tied his mount to the pony line, and walked over to the chuck wagon. Slocum handed him a plate of beans and beef, with a hot cup of joe. The strength of the open range coffee was a delight and Dan crouched near the men, savoring the brew.

"Trailing a ways?" asked Slocum.

"Tolerable amount, I guess." Dan finished the food and gave the plate to the wagon boss. "Great tasting grub, thank you."

"You bet. The Slash S chuck wagon never turns away a friendly stranger."

"The Slash S brand. Probably be your cattle been ranging west of here?"

"Chances good, Sweets seems to own most of everything around here."

Dan knew the signs of a long rider were still on him. The cowboys relaxing near the fire figured he was on the run from the law. Who else would be just riding through? While Dan's color was discussed some quietly, black men were not that unusual in this country, but they were still rare enough to stand out. This man, they saw had hard bark on him. Not a man to take lightly.

"Passed a homestead back a ways," said Dan, as he took time to build and light a smoke. "Woman and a couple of kids. Seems they been having trouble with your beefs crowding them." He heard the cowboys chuckling in a way that suggested, "Job well done." Seeds of anger began to grow in Pinkney's chest.

"That's a darn shame, there. Must be the Hilderbrant place. I been told she is a nice lady. Truth of the matter is, them people should have known better than to homestead near the only good water. Hard to keep these old critters from wandering up there, and they never care what they destroy. Hope they've caused no trouble for the purty lady."

"Thank you again for the grub," said Dan, "but I'm heading to town for supplies." He stood and backed away from the wagon toward his horse. He knew these were hard working cowboys. They were probably unheeled. He could not see any that wore guns, however a hidden weapon was just as deadly. He knew Slocum had a scatter gun in the food wagon. "Truth is, I wouldn't eaten here if I had known who you are. I've no respect for men who try to drive women and children out of their homes. Don't figure even rabid skunks would do that or speak lightly of it."

Dan's attention had been focused intently on the men around the chuck wagon. He hadn't heard the riders from the second shift coming in for chow. He first became aware of them as a lasso came sailing over his head and was pulled tight before he could react. The rope held his upper arms tight against his chest.

"Looks like I got me one of them homesteader lovers for Fiori. Y'all know how he loves them." There was laughing and a lot of comradery congratulations given to the man with the rope.

"Okay with you, Boss Slocum, I'll drag him back to the ranch now."

"Yep, take off, never deny Fiori his joys. Ride slow and if he's tough enough, he might still be alive when you get there."

The cowboy began backing his horse up, Dan pulled back against him as hard as possible, then suddenly relaxed. The force from the horse pulled him up into the air a little, and Dan rolled into a ball before he landed on the ground. His right hand slipped the Bowie knife from his boot sheath. He slashed through the rope, and continued his roll onto his feet. The horse stumbled with the load suddenly gone, and by the time the cowboy righted himself on the horse, Dan had stepped forward toward the man and with a long overhand toss, released the blade. The man jerked as the weapon hit him, then righting himself and looking downward, he could see the knife was buried hilt deep on the right side of his chest. With a puzzled look on his face, he slid backward off the horse and fell hard on his back.

Dan walked over to the downed man. "Maybe I oughta drag you back for Fiori. Serve you right, but I'd probably have to kill you and then him. So son, I want you to listen to me closely. Don't be looking over at your buddies. No one wants to die for you. Now the next time you want to rope someone, remember how much this hurt." Taking hold of his knife, he pulled it straight up out of the man's chest. Then slowly wiped the blade clean on the man's beard.

"Now you tried to kill me. I didn't try to kill you. Best remember that. Still, in a few weeks, you'll be feeling better and you'll start thinking, if I'd a had my gun, I'd have killed him. You wouldn't have, face it. You'd be dead now." Reaching down with his knife, he slashed a three inch gash across the man's face. "Every time you look in a mirror now, you'll realize how close you came. Next time I see that scar, I'll kill you flat out."

Replacing his knife in the sheath, he walked slowly back to his horse. He made sure he was facing Slocum and could see the other riders. He hadn't seen any sidearms, still he watched carefully. With his left hand, Dan released his mount from the pony line. Holding the reins lightly in his right hand, he drew his knife and the lariat forming their temporary corral. All their horses were free, but stood patiently waiting. He fired over them twice and they jerked around, pulling hard, then fled the campsite. "Funny how these old critters have their own mind," he said, and remounted. "Like I told you boys before, no real man battles women and kids. Best consider how much money you're making here, then think about how long you're going to be dead if I get angry. Way I see it, y'all would have let me drag to death. I'm good at remembering those kinda things. I'm looking at you Slocum."

Turning his horse straight east, he headed for town.

Boss Slocum

AS SOON AS The Kid left the camp with a flourish, Slocum grabbed the two cowboys next to him, "Bog, you and Tex, get over there and stop that idiot's bleeding. Drag him back here into the shade."

"Why didn't you use the shotgun on him? Know you always carry it in the chuck wagon," asked one of the cowboys.

"Who you think you're talking to? God dammit, get out there and catch them animals up. Get moving all of you, ain't no vacation going on here." He aimed a kick at the butts of the slow moving cowboys, making sure he missed widely.

"Damned fools couldn't see how far he stayed from me," Slocum said, talking to himself. "I couldn't kill him at that distance. The man knew what he was doing. If I'd a shot at him, best I could've done was hit him with a few buckshot. A man like that with no soul in his eyes could have killed us all."

One of the men came riding in, towing two more mounts.

"Bog, take him back to the ranch," he said, pointing at the wounded man. "Tell Mr. Sweets what's happened, and try to keep him alive," he said, pointing at the wounded man.

Ten minutes later, the man was off to spread the word to the main ranch.

"Just what we need, another range war, and this time with a man who knows how to fight," said Slocum. "Damn, what are you standing there watching for, get on that horse and round up the rest of them. Think you get paid for standing around and scratching?"

The man standing next to him caught up the horse and headed out.

Sweets' Ranch

CANDRAS SWEETS AND his wife Elva were sitting on the veranda when Bog rode in with the wounded man. He let the wounded man stay in his saddle while he ran up to tell his boss what had happened. Elva ran out to help the man down and led him up on the porch into the shade. She went into the house to get supplies to clean and treat the wounds.

"Sowbellied sun burnt son-of-a-bitch," Candras murmured under his breath. "Looks like that lady has picked up some help. This time, she's got a real man beside her." He looked up sharply at Bog, "Did Slocum get off a shot at him?"

"Nope. He was smart enough to stay just out of killing range."

"He could have at least wounded him. Let him know to stay out of our business."

Bog walked back to the bunkhouse shaking his head. Hellofa lot easier calling a play when someone else's life was on the line.

Sweets sent two messengers of his men off to Dry Creek. "Tell Fiori what's happened. If that sidewinder is still in town, kill him. If he's not there, tell Al to bring his men and get back here to the ranch. Don't spare your mounts, get there quick and tell him to ride fast."

When the men had left and Candras had sat back down, Elva turned to him, "I think you should tell me what is happening. Sounds to me like you're biting into something that should be left alone."

"Not now Elva, I've got some thinking to do."

"Well you better think about this. If you put pressure on a widow and two kids, you'll have half the country against you. That means they'll be against me. You dirty up my name and you'll have a tougher battle than you ever dreamed about."

"Shut up and let me think."

"You best watch your mouth, Candra. I'm treating a man with wounds on his face and chest, probably as a direct result of your hiring Fiori. How many more wounded or dead men do you want on your soul?"

Dry Creek

AFTERNOON HEAT MADE the sight of the town in the distance waiver and dance on the horizon. Dan rode into a small dusty town, a well-heeled stranger. Such men were always the focus of tongue and curiosity. The town had the familiar looks and smells of a hundred other towns he had ridden into. The few buildings, fronting Main Street, had long ago lost any paint that might have been applied. Riding past a saloon and eatery, he had turned into the livery stable, not wanting his mount to stand burdened in the hot sun as the dozen or so others were.

"Put him up for a couple of hours, and give him some grain. This big boy has earned it." he said to the liveryman.

"Ten cents extra for corn."

"Ya, that's okay," Dan said pulling the saddle off his mount and throwing it on the bales of straw stacked near the box. Walking back into the sun, standing quietly watching the town traffic, he built a smoke. The Kid was searching the faces of the men in the street looking for any hint of recognition. The training of a lifetime on the move taught him to assess carefully before exposing himself to undue danger.

A squat shaped man strolled past him, moving from the cool shade in the alley to the café across the street. Blond haired and nervous looking, he had the rolling, careless stride of a young man.

It seemed strange to Dan that there were so many riders in town. Working cowboys should have been out on the ranch working. Few ranchers paid men to hang around town. It worried him. He walked down the street a few doors to the sign announcing the general store.

A dour faced man smelling of mold stood behind the counter. Dan gave him his list of supplies, which the man carefully scratched on a piece of paper. Dan also picked up a few two-penny chocolate bars and a handful of hard candies that had a sign on them saying they were three for one penny and added the sweets to his order. He told the clerk he would be back in an hour.

"Cash on the barrelhead," the man said. "$13.63."

Dan gave him a twenty dollar bill out of his few remaining funds. "Throw in two boxes of those fifty caliber rounds. I got some hunting to do."

"Those will tear an antelope right in two," said the clerk.

"Ya, I like my antelope in two pieces," said Dan as he picked up his change.

"Give me a few minutes," the clerk said.

Dan walked down the street a few buildings to the sheriff's office. "Afternoon sheriff, I'm Sam Holliday," he said, giving the man the first name he could think of. "I'm looking for a man named Burt Hilderbrant. Passed by his homestead earlier, and his wife asked me to check. Seems he's a little late with the supplies."

The sheriff looked him over carefully. "Name is MacCaffee. The Hilderbrant's taken to hiring a black hand?"

"Mrs. Hilderbrant hired me to help until her husband comes back. That okay with you?"

"More than okay with me. Glad she's got someone to help. I got no axe to grind. But your man Hilderbrant isn't coming back. Killed last week. He's playing poker and got gunned down by a man named

Al Fiori. Buried him up on the hill. His widow wants the body, she'll have to come and get it. I got a package of his gear here somewhere. Wait just a minute," he said and walked to the back room of the building. He came back carrying a wrapped parcel. "Give that to the widow for me, please. Hilderbrant's horse and saddle is still at the livery. Tell them to send me the bill, no sense in saddling her with another bill. And a warning, a lot of the people in this town won't like to see a black man living out there, especially if he is living with a white woman."

"Mrs. Hilderbrant happens to be an upright Christian woman. People of the town ain't got any reason to judge her. They're not going to chase me off my job."

"And they shouldn't. If I can help with something, just let me know."

"That's a kindness, MacCaffee, still bad news for the widow," said Dan. "Hell, Burt didn't have much money. I wonder how he got in a poker game."

"Well mister, what did you say your name was, Holliday? Fiori is the foreman of the Sweets' ranch, everyone in this part of the country knows Sweets hates homesteaders, especially homesteaders who can limit Sweets access to water. I doubt there ever was a poker game. Fiori probably just shot him."

"That's the lay of it then. I kind of thought as much. So it will be the Slash S and their gunmen against Widow Hilderbrant and her two kids."

"Looking real bad for the widow. Not much I can do from here. I'm a town lawman, got no jurisdiction out there. When Hilderbrant was killed, every man in the bar claimed it was a fair fight. Course every man there worked for Sweets. If I arrested him, no jury would convict him anyway. Damn if I don't hate the way they're muscling her out of her home."

"Thank you MacCaffee, appreciate the news. I'm going to wash a little of this dust out of my mouth and then be heading back out to the homestead with supplies for her. Not looking forward to giving her the news."

"Don't buck those Slash S riders. There will be too many of them in there. They back you into pulling a gun, you going to lose. If you do win the fight, they'll testify against you and I'd hate to hang you."

"I'm listening to you, trust me, I'm like a little lamb."

Dan walked the dusty streets to the saloon. He counted roughly ten men, drinking, or clustered around a small stakes poker game. Dan moved up against the bar. Through the mirror, he could watch the men with their schemes and thoughts plain to him. He had spent his life dealing with men such as these. He knew someday his string of luck would end. There was a feeling of tension in the air. Something was planned against him. A feeling of white heat filled within him. He struggled to keep his poker expression. I've bought my way into a place with a weak spot that may well be the end of me. He tossed a silver dollar on the bar and ordered a whiskey.

Barman pulled down a bottle and filled a glass with whiskey, giving it to Dan. "Here you go mister. Two bits a shot." He went to make change, but Dan called him back.

"Give me a couple more shots, and several of those cigars."

Two full glasses appeared together with a couple of cigars.

"You be around long, mister?"

"That's my business, not yours."

"Making polite conversation is all," said the bartender and moved down to the other end of the bar. Dan noticed that several men left the bar after hearing his reply to the man.

A tall, heavily muscled man with a sour demeanor swept in the bar, four men followed in his wake. The man stood at the far end of the bar. His countenance was full angry, obviously he had been sent in to start a fight with Dan. If the man had been a bull, steam would have been coming out his nose. The Kid had missed nothing since walking in to the bar. Naturally a cautious man, being unaware when in the enemy's camp would have been an easy way to die swiftly. He assumed the men who were hanging around in a bar during the work-day would be Sweets' men.

The barrel chested man with a heavy beard was pumping himself up for a reason and Dan knew that he was the cause. Doubtful any of these bar bums were here to help him, chances seemed slim the man would be picking a fight with his saddle mates. Still, there was no apparent boss man, and The Kid couldn't pick out who was calling the play.

Still Dan stood quietly at the bar. He had lit a cigar and was work-ing on his third drink when Big and Mean complained to Vern, the bartender, about letting just anything walk into his bar. "Damned Indians should not be allowed to stink up a room with real men."

"Let him be, Harve, he's welcome to have a drink here as long as he's paying for it."

The rest of the men near the bar drifted away and sat at the tables near the door. Dan turned to face the man. He was outweighed by better than fifty pounds. Whatever happened now, he knew he couldn't let the man get a grip on him or his arms around him, too much muscle to defeat head on. He took off his hat and laid it gently on the bar.

"You gotta problem with me here, Fat Boy, you ought to talk to me."

"I'll talk to you then with these," he raised his fists up in a boxer's stance and charged at Dan with surprising speed.

The Kid flung his glass, still full of whiskey, at the man's face. It smashed into Harve's forehead right above his eye and whiskey colored with blood ran down into his eyes. It stopped the man and stood him up straight. Dan smashed his right fist against the man's face while his eyes were closed from the burning whiskey, and pushed the burning cigar at the big man's eyes. Harve took two steps back, got his balance back, and wiped the blood from his face. He smiled slowly at Dan, "Best you got?"

The force of Dan's punch throbbed all the way to his shoulder, he was out of drinks, and he obviously hadn't hurt Harve much.

"Better thrown at me than letting an Indian drink it," Harve said, and began another run at Dan.

Dan measured his enemy and crouching, threw a right that stopped Harve. Stepping closer, Dan rained punches to the man's gut, then to his face. Speed was his ally, but Harve threw a round-house that caught Dan below his right arm and smashed him into the bar. Knowing the strength and power his blows had on smaller men, Harve stepped back to let Dan fall, and was startled when the smaller man pressed the attack.

Dan was winded, and his ribs hurt with the power of Harve's blow. The man seemed impervious to any punches landed. Using the power of his legs, Dan leaped into the air at Harve, and as he descended, drove his forehead hard onto the man's nose driving him to his knees. Dan's head was exploding with pain and his hand still hurt from when he'd punched the big man.

Harve slowly struggled to his feet. Dan's boots were worn thin, but the leather in the toe was still thick and firm. Dan took one step then kicked at his opponent, now standing motionless. The kick shot the stiff piece of leather solidly into Harve's knee-cap, the weakest part of a fighting man's anatomy. A sickening sound filled the suddenly quiet bar as the knee exploded inward. Harve crashed forward, unable to move his injured knee to regain his balance.

Fear and pain filled his face. Of his many fights, none had gone anything like this. He was losing to the little man but still struggled to regain his feet, by pulling himself up with a chair. Dan waited patiently, stepping in when Harve was upright. He planted a solid right into the man's stomach followed by a savage uppercut.

This time the brutish man lay where he fell. No attempt to rise again.

Pinkney leaned back against the bar, surveyed the surprised faces glaring at him. "Anyone else got a problem with me drinking here?" He turned back to the bar and ordered another drink, and relit his cigar. Carefully picking up his hat and smoothing it, he placed it back on his head.

He heard the door open again. He heard a man call to him from behind but he didn't turn around. In the mirror, he could see a short grim man with narrow eyes and a tied down hog leg. Right behind him, MacCaffee entered the bar and took a chair at one of the tables.

"Hey you, I want to know how long you going to be around."

Dan knew it would be Fiori before he turned around to look at him: black hat, black gloves, pistol worn low and an evil gleam in his eye. Fiori must think he is special, thought Dan, as he turned back to his drink. Slowly he began to peel the gloves from his hands. They were a giveaway to a watchful man. His fingers were long and slim, covered with baby soft skin. Dan turned back to face Fiori but Fiori had turned toward MacCaffee.

"You butting into Slash S activities, MacCaffee? This ain't none of your business," Fiori said.

"Happens in town, it's my business. Anyone gets in a fight today, I'm the witness, not Sweets' paid-for men."

"I don't mind answering him, Sheriff MacCaffee. I assume he's the foreman out with Sweets. Well friend, I plan on finishing my drink here. Soon I will go down to get my supplies. After that, I'm riding out of town. That not okay with you, please let me know, cause you pull that hog leg of yours it will certainly slow me down some."

Fiori looked at the steel black eyes of The Kid, shot a quick look at MacCaffee, "Soon enough for me."

"This belong to you?" Pinkney was looking down at Harve who was just beginning to move.

"Yes, don't worry; we'll take care of him."

"Not worried at all, just inquisitive."

Back at the general store, Dan strapped the supplies to Burt's horse, glad now that he hadn't brought a supply horse. The extra horse would slow him down some and the way this town was breaking might find him needing to ride in a hurry. He bought four more cans of peaches and several extra cigars for himself. He started to leave then went back and returned with two boxes of 30-30 cartridges for Burt's rifles. He was down to less than fifty dollars now, but with luck that should last him to the west coast.

Once in the clear, he kicked his mount up to a canter and headed back to the homestead. "Tarnation and Beelzebub's breathe, what the hell am I doing? I think that peckerwood broke a couple of my ribs. The law is after me, there must be thirty guns riding for that Sweets' pepperbox and here I am carrying candy back to a homestead. They all seem to want to rub me out. Maybe I best drop the supplies on her and head out."

Three days later, Jake Andly rode into town, leading a horse carrying the wounded Sheriff Steel.

The Posse

SHERIFF STEEL AND Andly had ridden due west. The flat prairie with its patches of spicy sage mixed in with the long grasses seemed to run on forever. During the first week, they had run across signs of The Kid several times, but had lost his trail.

The long prairie they were riding through looked flat, extending as far as they could see in all directions. But its flatness was an illusion causing the men that rode through it to believe they were safe. With no windbreaks, the grass always seemed to be blowing and the movement of the small bushes and high grasses prevented the human eye from seeing any undulations in the land itself. Any clouds overhead had the effect of changing the light hitting the ground and the alternating darker and lighter shades hid the small hills and arroyos. The heat beating down was a significant part of the visual deception, the waves of warm air reflecting the light out made layers of shining air look like waves of water floating over the surface. These unconscious eternal forces acted on the rider's eyes and relaxed his brain. Steel and Andly believing they could see everything clearly had relaxed their constant vigil and readiness.

The small band of Ute Indians rode out of a small undulation on the prairie, less than fifty yards from the lawmen. The Utes were possibly as surprised as the men, but alert and ready for deer and antelope, they saw the men at once and figured they could easily take the men's horses. They immediately attacked. This was a hunting party and although several had rifles, most carried their bows. The traditional method for hunting was still preferred over the newer use of firearms.

Steel and Andly whirled on their horses and raced directly away from the band, searching wildly for any cover they could find, while the occasional bullet or arrow buzzed the air above them. Steel saw a buffalo wallow twenty yards ahead, pointed it out to Jake and the two reined in their mounts, shook their feet free and slid from the saddles. They forced the horses to lie down, trying to protect them from injury. The wallow gave them less than a foot of protection. Still it was the best they could do with the Indians closing on them rapidly.

"Looks to be a hunting party," said Steel. "Aim for their horses. They're probably looking to pick off our mounts, but the loss of a few of theirs might change their minds. Riding in with a couple extra horses will give them big medicine."

Lying flat in the depression, with Andly holding the mounts down, Steel, crouching and peering over the embankment, began shooting at the small band. They immediately turned and retreated out of rifle range.

"Let me see that buffalo rifle of yours," Steel said to Andly. Chambering the two inch long shell, he began to steady himself, drew in three or four deep breaths then blew the air out of his lungs. He gently took aim and slowly squeezed off the round. The scream of a wounded horse filled the air as he watched it writhe wildly then go down.

The Utes fired back wildly amidst the chaos, while Steel chambered another round. The silence in the wallow was contrasted against the shouts of the Indians. Suddenly as a group, they raced directly back at the men, firing their rifles and aiming arrows high into the air to arc down on the pinned men.

Steel's next shot took the lead horse in the throat. The force of the round lifted the animal up onto his rear legs and then over to one side, throwing the brave on his back rolling to one side. The thrashing hooves and the smell of blood panicked the other mounts and broke the charge. His rider leaped onto the back of another horse, and the band raced out of sight in the waving grass.

"In the name of Bess, they were fast," said Jake, "I thought they had us for sure. At least they backed off for a ways. Now what?"

"Well first off, I suppose you ought to get this arrow out of my leg."

One of the arrows had pierced Steel's upper thigh. Its shaft was sticking about a foot out of the back of his leg. Turning him over, Jake saw the arrowhead emerging three inches.

Jake slit the sheriff's pant leg up above the wound and cut the cloth free. He tore it into long strips and laid the long pieces of cloth on Steel's stomach. "Hold on now, cause we gotta get it out. Probably going to hurt a tad."

The first part was easy, he broke off the arrowhead emerging from the front of Steel's leg. He broke open several of his .50 cal. rounds and poured the powder out onto one of the strips of cloth. He rolled the strip and tied it to the broken end of the arrow. He grasped the feathered shaft and pulled the arrow almost out. He fired the gun powder strip, waited for the count of three, and pulled everything out of the wound. Blood still leaked a little from the leg. Jake quickly stuffed pieces of cloth into the wound to staunch the flow of blood, then tied the remaining strips around the leg holding the bandages in tight. Hopefully the heat cauterized the wound and would prevent an infection.

The sheriff with his eyes closed and fists clenched hard against the pain, lay silently for several minutes. "You're a cold-blooded bastard, Andly."

"I know. Hope we can save that leg."

Jake stood and surveyed the area, "Can't see them anywhere. Your choice Ernie, wait till dark or ride now. If they're crawling at us in the grass, we won't see them until they're right on us."

"Let's ride now," said Steel. "Two of them are on foot or riding double. Hopefully they won't want to chase us."

Getting the horses up, he helped the sheriff into his saddle. They rode straight west away from the Utes, as rapidly as they could with the sheriff holding his reins in both hands while he also gripped the saddle horn to stay mounted.

They had a short, restless night, and by morning, Steel's leg had swollen badly. It looked to be twice the size of normal. They ate quickly with the sheriff barely able to sit up.

"We're swimming round in pickle juice here," said Jake. "No way can you ride a saddle with that leg, and if we wait here, we'll run out of water in a day or two. The mountains look closer now, and it could be there's a town just ahead, but I've seen no signs of life. No travelers or cattle anywhere."

"Blamed bad luck," said the sheriff. "Hope those Indian bastards roast in the ninth layer of hell. I been thinking on our troubles myself. Best chance we got is you scouting ahead. Mayhaps you'll find a town or a ranch with a buckboard, so I can get out of here."

"I'm thinking you're dead on. Can't go back, and can't move us both right now. Hate to leave you cause of the heat and the Indians, but we gotta do something. And it might just as well be now." He threw his extra canteen to the sheriff, mounted his horse and rode west.

He tailed straight for a while, then began to zigzag northerly, then southerly, hoping he would see more ground that way. Worrying about the wounded man, he rode faster than he wanted and he was tiring his horse quicker than he knew was wise. He just couldn't force himself to ride slower.

Near noon, he found a small creek that was still running. Dismounting, he pulled the saddle off his mount to let it cool and rest. He drank deeply himself, then filled his canteen. The horse was grazing on the short lush grass growing on the banks, and he let it rest and feed to regain strength.

He sat with his back against a tree, closing his eyes for a few minutes. He pulled out his makings and lit a smoke. The shade and sound of the running water were soothing after the hard days across the prairie. Watching the new growth of aspen trees flashing their leaves in the slight breeze gave him the idea. Soon he was up and hacking at the base of a tree with his knife. Cutting down two of the saplings, he tied their trunks together. He brought his horse over, saddled it, tied a drag line on the trees, and began riding back to the sheriff.

Steel was unconscious when Andly made it back. Jake formed a travois out of the aspens, then used leaved branches and saddle blankets to form a nest. He pulled and pushed Steel on the travois while he was still unconscious, and tied him to the aspens to prevent him sliding off. Slowly he began the trip back to the creek.

Sweets' Ranch

SWEETS WAS PACING his veranda with a glass of whisky in his hand and an open bottle sitting on a small stand, when Fiori and his gunhands rode up.

While the men walked off, Fiori approached Sweets. He had never seen the old man this upset, but Al was unshaken. He was the big honcho here, not a lowly cow chasing foreman.

Sweets had spent the time since the wounded man had been brought in, running over the turn of events. He had regretted hiring Fiori many times, as the man became more powerful. Now he was glad to have the foreman here with his gunhands. The strength of this widow Hilderbrant had not been in his playing hand. Fiori was a warrior and would help him secure his range, his water, and soon Sweets would own the town. It had been easy enough to run the other homesteaders and a couple of the ranchers off. He would not let one woman backed only by a half-breed defeat him.

"Did you kill that man?" he asked Fiori.

"Couldn't, he had left town before I found out you wanted him killed. Sent a couple of men after him, but it was getting too dark to track him."

"That black son of a bitch wounded one of our men at the branding camp. Half the cowboys are spooked."

"Them cattle hands are always spooked. Don't worry about them too much, soon as we get rid of him, things will be back to normal. I saw him in town. He beat Harve senseless. I didn't think anyone could do that. I was going to kill him on principle, but MacCaffee came in the bar. Didn't think you wanted a war with the town as yet, so I chased him out of town and told him to keep moving."

"Well, sounds like you did about as good as you could anyway. That MacCaffee better keep his nose out of our business."

"Why does this one guy worry you so much?"

"Gotta bad feeling about him, I want you to put a couple of men out there watching the homestead, and soon we'll figure a way to ambush that black son of a sidewinder. I know we gotta kill him."

"This Pinkney is going to be one tough hombre. When you start this war, be ready for a real battle. I've seen him fight up close. He's half puma and half grizzly. He is going to take a whole lot of killing."

"That's why I have you here. You want to run that town, we gotta get rid of the homesteaders."

"We'll kill him fast enough. Not something for you to worry about. Pour me a glass of that whisky. I'll send out watchers in the morning."

Anne

IT HAD BEEN another long hot day, with Dan absent from the homestead. At last the sun began to hide behind the mountains and the air began to cool perceptively. She had pulled a chair out onto the porch enjoying the small breeze drifting through the valley. Adam and Jewel were playing a throw game with sticks and a large circle they had drawn in the dirt. Earlier she had been able to draw water for the horses and had pulled down enough hay to last the night.

She saw Dan approaching from the south, riding slowly and leading a horse. "Poor man," she thought, "He is so alone. Seems this side of the world is out to beat him down, but this place is so much better with him here." She recognized the spare horse and saddle he was leading. Knew instantly what news he was bringing. He dismounted in the yard, led the horse up to the porch and began unfastening the supplies. Stacking the cornmeal, flour, and bacon on the porch, he handed a package tied with string to the woman. He unloaded the last two packages and put them to the side.

"Bad news, Mrs. Hilderbrant. Should be I could say it better, but I'm not that good with words. Burt was killed in Dry Creek. That package is what the sheriff gave me. I know you recognize his horse and saddle."

She tore the package open, pulling out his hat and boots, a sidearm, and his rifle. "Not much for a lifetime is it?"

"Probably as much as most men have. We're not big on owning things that can't fit on a horse. Can't ride with it, most feel they don't need it," said Dan.

"Adam, come here for a minute, would you?" she called.

When he ran over, she told him to dig a good sized hole behind the cabin, and walked back into the cabin. Minutes later, she came out carrying what clothes and things Burt had left behind. Slowly she carried them to where Adam was digging.

When the hole was deep enough, she slowly threw Burt's things in, one at a time. Keeping only his sidearm and rifle, the rest was buried as she helped Adam fill the hole back in.

"Done with him and his," she said, backing off and dusting her hands. "He is gone now and will be quickly forgotten."

She returned to the porch and sat in the chair. Dan having taken care of the horses was sitting on the steps to the porch and enjoying a smoke. She looked at him quietly. "You probably think that's harsh but I will never look back on that man with a pleasant thought. Just glad he's gone, never to return."

In the silence that followed, she believed she knew men well enough to judge the man sitting with her. She wanted him to stay with her forever. He was a good man, strong, and with deep currents running through him. She also believed that she could be the woman for him. If he stayed with her, it would be a life of hard work, and disappointments, but it would also be a life of affection and togetherness. She felt she could be the rock he built his life on.

'What about my life has caused me to lose everything?" she asked.

He did not, could not, answer her. Dan sat quietly in thought, wrapped up hard in the complexity of what life would be here: the kids, the horses, a need for money, and a steady income to keep the place going. He was not the type of man who had dealt with such thoughts. His life had been lived out under a different star. His life had been spent always moving. Life had begun with a difficult birth and he figured it would always end in action. Reckless, carefree, loose women, whiskey, and a life spent balancing himself on the next roll of the dice was gone forever.

She broke the tension of the moment, "Time I fixed us some chow. You gotta be empty and I expect them kids could do justice to a biscuit or two."

The kitchen was cleaned, children tucked in and sleeping. The night was cool and Lugunea could hear the breeze blowing steadily against the cabin. She walked out to the porch, where Dan was still sitting watching the night. He was finishing up one of his store bought cigars.

"Evening, Mrs. Hilderbrant," he said, "picked up something for you at the store today." He stood and with a little flourish, handed her a small, white foiled square.

She sat down next to him, opened her present, a chocolate bar, broke off a small bit and put it in her mouth. She broke another bit off, and held it to his lips, "Taste this," she said.

"Mmm, chocolate," Dan said. "Not much better in this world than chocolate."

"It tastes even better to me." The soft glowing coals of the cook stove gently lit her face. Dan could see the softness of her face and the deep green emerald of her eyes. "Want to know why it tastes so good to me?"

"Yes, I would."

"This is the first present anyone ever bought for me. No one ever liked me enough to buy me a gift before. Much less anything that tastes as good as chocolate."

"I am happy you like it, Mrs. Hilderbrant."

"Dan, my first name is Lugunea," she said. "Please don't call me that. My middle name is Anne. That's what I go by. I want you to call me Anne. I never want to be called Mrs. Hilderbrant again. I hated that name and that man."

"Anne it is, and Anne I will call you. But you don't know me very well. Before we travel too far down a path together, I want you to know a little about me. If'n you can't abide me, I would understand. I'm known on the trail as The Cherokee Kid. I am not liked by many, and there's some I had to kill. My mother was a slave owned by a Cherokee Indian. Manala, my mother, never told me who my father was. She died on the Trail of Tears, a freed woman, who was worked to death by the tribe. I was taken in by an Indian family who raised me. I've been riding the lone trail since I was sixteen. Right now, I am on the prod. There's a posse behind me searching to bring me back to South Dakota. If I stay too long with you, they'll catch me sure."

"Dan, look at me, will you? You know only too well that I like you and am grateful to you." Dan looked down at her upturned face. She was beautiful with emerald green eyes that seemed to see into his soul. "You want to walk down a path together, I will walk next to you proudly. I would boast to tell the world, you're my man."

"Anne with the beautiful eyes, you've owned my affections since first I saw you. But why would you consider being with an ordinary galoot like me?"

"Dan Pinkney. Don't you never no more, ever say something like that to me. I'm looking at those droopy, old eyes and that huge brush of a mustache, and I'm thinking you're the most beautiful man I ever did see. More than that, when I'm with you, I feel safe. I know me and the kids will always be okay while you're with us."

"Will you dance with me, Anne?"

"For as long as you want, Dan."

He held out his left hand and she moved into his embrace, encircling his body with her right arm and pulling him close. He could feel the heat as her body pressed against him. The smell of her hair and the feel of her strength with the movement of her back were intoxicating. He began a slow two-step dance to a song long remembered and she moved smoothly, step by step with him. He found himself humming an old melody.

Annie's hand moved to his face and brought his head down to hers for a first kiss. At first startled, he pulled back, then gently leaned forward and kissed her in return.

"Stay with me tonight. I've spent my life searching for you, now you are here," she said lowly to him.

"Did you hear me? The law may drag me away tomorrow."

"Then Dan, my love, we'll have had this night to keep us warm with memories."

"The kids will hear us."

"That's the way with kids. Sometimes they hear, sometimes they sleep. Either way, they'll just know how much I love you."

He had been with women before, but only cheap bar room women he purchased when his needs were strong. Never had he been with a woman who wanted him. She was magical and soft.

Her dress seemed to fall from her shoulders, hurrying him to unfasten his clothes and join her as she sat on the edge of the bed. She pulled him to her and gently guided him until he was in her.

She clutched at his back, bit his shoulder lightly and while Dan was still caught up in the beauty of the moment, Anne came to an abrupt halt with a soft moan. She held him tight and motionless, clutching him tightly with her legs.

Dan felt his heart twist sideways in his chest and she was pulling him closer still. "You are indeed a fine man," she whispered as they caressed gently before sleeping.

In the morning, with the larder refurbished, Anne cooked a wonderful breakfast for the four of them.

Later, with steaming cups of coffee, Dan talked to Anne on the porch as they watched the children play.

"It's going to start in earnest now, Sweets and Fiori know I'm here. As long as I am here to help you, they know you won't leave. From what the sheriff in Dry Creek told me, Mr. Sweets is dead centered on clearing the homestead out of this valley. He thinks he needs the water for his cattle. I don't know the actual count of the men against us, but there will be bunch more than just you and me. I'm not trying to scare you or tell you what to do, but if you choose to leave, I will go with you. If you choose to stay, I will stay with you, as long as I can."

"We'll stay. This is our place. I refuse to be chased from it."

"You got a lotta iron in you, girl. I truly admire it."

"I think we gotta give those horses a little run and some fresh grass to eat. I'm taking out, be back in an hour or two." Dan got his horse ready, opened the corral gates and took the horses out. After their long confinement, he had to force several of them to join the pack. With his horse and a length of rope carried in his right hand, he managed to keep them in a tight group. The natural mentality of horses was to group together in the herd. He rode them north, and near the first of the small creeks, he let them graze on the rich grasses and drink from the snowmelt still running down from the mountains. Seeing that they weren't interested in moving much, he rode the area around him searching for signs of danger. Long familiar with reading tracks he soon found a small patch of grass near the creek where several horses had spent time. The grass had been cropped short, telling him that riders had spent time waiting. No campfires, no discarded materials, why would they have stopped here?

Looking back over the valley, he could just make out the cabin. A man with a telescope or binoculars would have been able to see every move made on the homestead.

Rounding the horses up, he trotted them back to the corral. They handled easily, Dan was sure Burt had worked with them in the same way.

He sat on the porch and took out his makings pouch and made a smoke. When Annie came out to sit with him, he said, "We need to talk Anne. I had a little fracas with the Slash S yesterday, wounded one of them. That was before I got to town. It was something they pushed on me, but I'm pretty sure it will be laid at my door.

"Another thing you should know is that the foreman of Slash S is the guy that pushed Burt into a fight so's he could kill him.

"I think they are coming soon. They mean to push you out of the country. They want this valley for themselves.

"Now this is your place, sorry if I hurried their hand, but that's the lay of it as I see it."

"I'm not leaving Dan. I will fight them to stay here. This is my place, my only place, and I'm not leaving." He could hear the steel in her voice, the determination in what she said. Then he heard a sob and looked back over his shoulder to see her whole frame shaking as she held her hands to her eyes. Quickly he rose and took her in his arms.

"Of course this is your place. You made the choice and you know I am with you. Now stop that sobbing, it's just wasting time. We gotta make us some plans here about how we are going to beat them. We just have to make it too hard and too costly to keep battling us.

"I believe their first foray against us will be soon, but they are so confident in their numbers they won't bring many men and they'll be careless. After that, we'll talk about this again. You know that we can fight and be stubborn, but we just got to make sure them little tykes are safe," said Dan.

"I don't know what I would do without you. I'm backing any move you make. This place is yours as much as it is mine. You already know that I am a shameless woman where you are concerned. I want you and the kids want you."

The Cherokee Kid

BEFORE THE DARK had broken, with the help of a half-moon to ride by, Dan left the homestead and rode to the creek where he had taken the horses to graze the previous day. Taking his .44 cal. rifle with six extra cartridges from his horse, he turned the horse loose and slapped it on the butt, knowing it would return home.

"Let's just see if these dinkwoods are fools enough to return."

Heritage and training had all senses on full alert. Carefully tasting the air trying to pick up any unnatural sounds or smells in the area, struggling to stay awake, he picked up a small pebble and put it in his mouth. His mind wouldn't let him slip into sleep as long as the smooth object was in his mouth. Digging himself deep into the brush and cover on the banks of the creek, laying his rifle in front of him, he chambered a round, relaxed a little. He again rechecked the load in his pistols as he waited.

As first light fought its way west, he heard the creak of a saddle. Shortly thereafter, he saw shadows moving into their former positions near the creek. The quiet of the mesa was now broken by the cropping sounds of the horses grazing. Not a loud sound to be sure, but against the total silence, it was unmistakable.

As the sun's light filtered in more, he located two men by their low talking. The boredom of a quiet watch of a distant cabin had driven the men to conversation. Dan couldn't make out what they were say-ing, but it was their hiding place he was able to find, not needing the latest gossip. Slowly, he withdrew himself from the brush and stood against a tree. If they had looked his way, they wouldn't have picked him out with his dark shape pressed against the black of the tree.

They were still ahead of him a good twenty yards as he was clos-ing the distance slowly, when his foot found and broke a dry branch lying on the ground.

"What was that?" asked one of the men.

"Horses going down for a drink. You getting to be jumpier than a fox in heat," said the other.

"Well, I don't like it. I didn't sign on to stand watch behind a bunch of trees. Figured when I came there'd be action, and I mean gunpow-der action against men. This pushing against a lady and two kids, it's just wrong."

"Don't let Fiori hear you say that. He'll beat your ass all over the ranch, then fire you. Best shut up and do what you're told."

Dan stepped silently out of the thicket with his rifle aimed at the men. He recognized the squat blond haired kid from town. He hadn't seen the other man around. They both looked at and then past him, as if they hadn't recognized he really was standing with a gun pointed at them.

"Hope you been listening to your buddy there, cause if you listen to me real good, you just might live through this. First, drop those binoculars." The man on the right looked over at the blond man.

"You holding a single shot rifle there mister. You fire it and we'll kill you."

"Could be you saying it right, but one of you'll have a hole big as Kansas in your chest. Now drop the glasses or make a play."

The glasses hit the ground.

"Now, get your hands up and be quick about it, cause I ain't et yet and I'm a touch irritated about having to come out here so early."

Both men lowered their hands down near their guns.

"You ain't going to shoot," the blond man said, as Dan stepped forward and smashed him in the mouth with the barrel of the Sharp. Whirling, with his rifle held straight out, he hit the other man across the bridge of his nose with the barrel. The cowboy had been drawing his pistol, but had not cleared leather before he was knocked off his feet with the force of the blow.

Dan saw Blondie begin to draw his gun and took a step toward him, hitting the shorter man flush on the side of his head with his right fist. The gun discharged into the ground as Blondie fell unconscious looking like a sack of sand in the filtering shadows. Dan took both sidearms and threw them behind him.

The blond man's legs began to shake, like maybe he was trying to stand up. Dan, never all that patient, tapped him on the head with the gun's barrel. Blondie lay still again. Dan flipped him over, and tied the man's hands behind his back with a cord. Walking to the other man, not sure if he was still alive, Dan could see blood bubbling from his mouth as he tied to breath. Dan tied the man's hands behind him. He pulled both men to their feet, walked them out of the thicket to clear ground, and threw them back on the ground.

"You are two sad looking pistoleros," he said. "If this had been a shooting war, you'd both be dead before you could get your weapons out. Now let's talk. I want to know what plans Sweets and Fiori have for Mrs. Hilderbrant. The one who talks first will get to ride out of here."

The two young men looked at each other, then back at Dan. They weren't talking.

"Uh oh, lads, looks like we got a bad case of stubborn here." He pulled the hat off each man and walked back down to the creek, threw both hats in, and walked back to the men.

"Hope you didn't like those hats. Personally, they looked like they came out the back end of a cow, and a sick cow at that. Now let's try that question and answer game again. What plan does Fiori and Sweets have for Mrs. Hilderbrant?"

Still nothing from the men.

He went back to the men and catching the blond man's leg, began to pull his boot off. Blondie tried to kick him with his other leg, but Dan stepped back and kicked him in the genitalia. "Probably not wise to try to kick a man who has you tied up," he offered, pulling the boots off the now quiet man. The other man offered no resistance and soon both were bootless.

"Last chance for you songbirds. Either of you want to ride back yet?"

Nothing.

"Okay, you first Blondie, we gonna have a private talk." Dan pulled him to his feet and taking baby steps, walked him out of sight down by the stream. Once they were alone, Dan removed the man's bandanna and gagged him. He began asking questions, "How many men does Sweets have? What's Sweets plan for the homestead?" After each question, Dan whacked a nearby tree with a stout limb. "You just ain't going to talk are you?" Dan picked up a large rock and tossed it into a deep part of the creek. "You don't talk, I got no use for you." The blond man wriggled and squirmed hard against his bindings, but a small tap with Dan's pistol settled him right down.

The Kid walked back to the other bound man. "Looks like it's up to you, Sunshine. Same questions while you consider whether you want to walk or swim back to the ranch. How many men does Fiore have?"

"There's thirty three at the ranch, fifteen of us are under Fiori."

"What's his plans for the Hilderbrant homestead?"

"He's never said, but I think he wants us to watch so he will know what to expect when he attacks. He's determined to get rid of all the homesteaders."

"Good decision," said Dan. He cut the man's bindings. "You can head on back to the ranch."

Dan went to the blond man and cut him loose. ""I know you stupid and strong as a chunk of wood, but you hang around long enough,

I'm just naturally going to have to kill you. By the time you get back to the ranch, you'll understand that actions have consequences, and perhaps you'll even understand the difference between mouth and means." The man hurried to catch up with the other watcher and the two walked off, hatless and bootless, in the direction of the Slash S ranch.

Putting their pistols and the binoculars into the saddlebags, he mounted one of the horses and leading the other, headed back toward the cabin. Halfway back, he stopped and cut the cinch of the saddle for the animal he was leading, and turned it loose. It trotted off, heading south. The saddle bounced loosely on its back for a while, then fell onto the mesa. Losing his saddle and weapons would be a devastating loss to a cowboy.

He finished the ride to the cabin, tied the horse up to the corral, and walked into the cabin just in time for breakfast.

"Lordy, Lordy, your cooking smells wonderful," he told Anne.

After eating, he pulled two chairs out onto the porch so Anne could sit with him while he watched the children at play.

"Oh my goodness," he said, standing and walking to his saddle. "I'm getting more forgetful all the time." He pulled out the package of hard candies and returned to his chair. Sharing with Anne what he had purchased, he said, "I think they'll really like these."

"You're right, they'll jump through hoops for those," said Anne.

"Jewel, Adam," he called, "can you come here for a minute?" They looked at him suspiciously, wondering if there was a chore involved.

"You'll like this," he called, and when they were on the porch, he let them take their pick of the highly colored candies. They sat on the porch steps to eat their treats.

"What do you say?" asked their mother.

The kids turned and looked at her blankly.

She explained, "When someone gives you something, you're supposed to say 'thank you'."

"Thank you, Dan," they both chimed.

Dan gave the package to Anne. "Do you want one?"

"Of course I do, but let's save them for treats. Look, the kids really love them."

"I want to tell you what's happening, so you'll have the full story."

"Figured something was up when your horse came in alone. Next thing I know, you're riding in on a strange horse."

"Crap, better let him go," said Dan. He walked over to the animal, took the saddle and bridle off the animal, letting it wander free. The animal walked around a bit, sniffed the horses in the corral, then ran off to the east. "He'll be home pretty quick. Don't want to be known as a horse thief.

"Yesterday when I was grazing our horses down by the creek, I saw a worrisome thing. Someone had been letting their animals crop the grass by the creek. It was suspicious because there was nothing else there. I figured it couldn't be someone just passing through cause they'd have left a campsite.

"I went out early this morning and set up a watch. Caught a couple of Slash S riders watching the cabin with binoculars. I sent them on back to Sweets' Ranch without their horses. They got messed up a bit, but they'll be okay. Not sure if Sweets is going to retaliate or not."

"Next time, tell me ahead of time, Dan. I was terrified when your horse rode in. I thought I'd lost you."

Dan looked down and shook his head. "I just wasn't thinking. I'm sorry. Probably too many years alone to think of others first. I will try. So today, I'm going to be riding the hills above us. Those two got me a little worried, gotta find out if there's a site up above where they could ambush us. I feel we need to know the land above us. Then later, I plan on riding back to Dry Creek. The sheriff there is named MacCaffee and he seems like a straight up guy. He'll let me let me know if there's a bad brew boiling against us."

"Promise me you'll come back to us."

"I will always come back to you. I ain't letting no one or nothing snatch this piece of paradise away from me. I'll be close all morning, so if something happens this morning, fire off your rifle twice and I will hurry back. Later you'll be on your own and that eats at me. Stay in the cabin if anyone comes and you should be safe. If I didn't think I had to, I wouldn't leave you alone ever."

"I'm tougher than I look, Dan, and I'm a good shot. I know you gotta do some things, so get them done and return to us."

She turned his face to hers and kissed him. "Remember what's waiting for you here and that I love you. Now hurry and get your riding done."

Saddling up one of Annie's horses, to give his mount a rest, he rode upward behind the cabin. Soon he was following crossing game trails as he searched the hills and valleys behind the cabin.

He rode slowly in the coolness of the trees covering a semi-circle of about three miles while staying deeply hidden by the forest. He searched out places where shooters would have a good view of the cabin, but saw no sign that others had been there. In one valley, he found a large dry cave with its entrance almost covered with brush. A small creek trickled down the valley near it. It would be a good hidey hole if the worst came to worst, a safe place for Anne and the kids if a range war came to them.

His reconnaissance done, he rode the mountain toe down to the mesa. Figuring he was some north of town, he put the horse into a canter to eat up the distance quickly. He'd picked a good mount; it had heart and stamina to spare.

Picking up the outline of the town off to his left, he slowly entered, walking the horse down the main street. He tied up to the hitching post in front of the sheriff's office with enough slack left in the reins that the pony would be able to drink from the trough.

Sheriff MacCaffee was seated behind his desk rifling through papers when Dan walked in.

"Hello Mr. Pinkney," he said.

"You got my real name from someone," said Dan.

"A deputy from South Dakota brought in the wanted poster yesterday. He's asking if I'd seen you."

"What did you tell him?"

"Not much. South Dakota warrant doesn't mean a pinch of snuff out here, but there's a lot of people in town. Some good ones and some bad. I wanted to tell you so you could be prepared either way."

"Reward doesn't interest you?"

"Dan, you've been upstanding since you came to the area. Don't know any bad men as would take the side of a widow and two kids against those ranchers. I know you've been pressed by the Slash S, and I know he's madder than hell at you. But that's not my worry now, is it? Seems like you could have killed a couple of them and not been too far out of line. Still, I'm the town sheriff and I take care of the law in town. As to the reward, I wouldn't take you away from the Hilderbrant homestead and leave that family alone for nothing, certainly not a measly five hundred dollars.

"Just so's you know, Sheriff Steel from Belle Fourche is up in the hotel with a bad leg. Arrow got him out on the prairie. Be a while 'til he's back on two feet. The deputy is another matter though, and he's still sniffing around for you."

"Sounds like you're a pretty upstanding man yourself, MacCaffee. I like a man with sand."

"That's me; poor, underpaid, underappreciated government worker who will probably die broke. Still, when I go, I want to go with a clear conscience when I meet my maker," said MacCaffee.

"The problem I came to see you about, before you threw the heavy logs on the fire, is them kids. Don't know the type of man Sweets is, but if the Slash S comes against me with guns, I figure I got it coming. Mrs. Hilderbrant is there to battle for her place, but I gotta find sanctuary for the tykes," said Pinkney.

"Well, right offhand, I'd say you could leave them with widow Griffin. She's a southern lady who runs the eatery. She won't like you cause you're black. She's expressed her hatred of blacks and mixed races since coming to town. But the kids are a different story. She'd guard them with her life and she's supported by most everyone in town. If you leave them with her, I'll be watching them too. You got my word on it."

"Your word is gospel to me. Don't know why them southerner's hate me so much. They's the ones sent the Cherokees on the Trail of Tears which resulted in my mother death. You'd think I'd be the one to hate them instead of the other way around," said Pinkney.

"Some people get lost in time, can't see the reality of today. There ain't nothing you can do for them but feel sorry. Now when you leave, you'd be wise to go out through the alley and ride out of town the back way. Deputy won't see you that way."

"I'll do my best not to let the trouble boil into your town, Sheriff, and thanks for all your help."

Jake Andly

STANDING QUIETLY IN the bar, listening and watching the townsmen milling about, Andly had learned more about Dry Creek in three days than he knew about Belle Fourche after living there several years. These Montana Territorial townspeople liked to talk. Any news or gossip was sure to draw a crowd of people ready to speak their minds. It seemed to Jake, that as long as they were in the safety of the bar with friends, and the less they knew about something, the longer they talked it, and the more certain they were of their conclusions.

Tonight, Dave Vegas, one of the local men, was holding forth on the incompatibility of the races. God has created the Indians, the black men, and the whites so different, that he could not have wanted them to live together." He had three or four other men listening to him. "Now we have a half-breed, black Indian man, working out on the Hilderbrant homestead, with no one else around. We have to protect this white woman from this man. He obviously has her under a powerful spell."

The bartender, Vern, finally had his fill of the stupidity of the ranting. "Just what the hell business is it of yours? Why you want to talk bad about a man who is helping the Hilderbrant woman? That man seems an upright kind of guy. Who else would go against the Slash

S? That's a helluva lot more than you would do, Dave Vegas. In fact, there ain't no one in this town willing to help her. This town is scared of Sweets. They would let those kids starve to death and never lift a hand. And you Vegas, you're hardly taking care of your own family as it is, and you haven't got Al Fiori riding against you."

"What business you got talking me down, Vern, you fat tub of horse crap?"

"I'm tired of you flapping hate and unrest around town especially against a guy who is just trying to help someone. Seems like you spent more time earning a living and feeding your kids better, and less time talking stupid, you' be better off. And I might be a fat turd, but I earn my own way. Now I'm the fat tub of horse crap telling you to get the hell out of my bar."

A cold, hard look was in Dan Vegas as he backed away from the bar. The tight grip of fear in his belly overrode his anger at the bartender, and he turned and walked out of the swinging doors, accompanied by calls of, "About time you got rid of him," from the other townsmen at the bar.

"Damn, I thought he was going to pull his piece," said Jake.

"Naw," said the man next to him, "Vegas was born a worm and will die a worm's hard death."

"Who is this Mrs. Hilderbrant?" Jake asked casually, "Seems she's in some big trouble."

"I'll say, woman has a homestead twenty miles west of here and the big ranch, the Slash S, is putting a squeeze on her. I think they want to get her water rights. Her husband got killed at that table over there less than a month ago."

The bar's door swung open and Dan Vegas came running in with his gun drawn. The bartender, Vern, fired his pistol through the doors, at least a foot over the man's head. Vegas heard the pistol roar and dropped to the floor like he'd been shot in the heart. Vern walked over to where the motionless figure lay. "Don't do that again Dave, I'm not a good shot and you could get killed by accident. Now you get on back home. See you tomorrow if you can keep your idiot babble in your head."

Vegas stood slowly. "Sorry Vern, I guess I got too wound up," he murmured, wandering back into the night.

Jake stretched and finished his drink. "Time for me to head out too," and strolled out of the bar. Ten minutes later, he had his mount saddled and was heading west. Jake was a taciturn man. Watchful and careful, he stopped his horse several times, and backtracked to listen for any pursuit. He always watched his trail no matter where he rode. He was hunting the most dangerous of prey and he knew getting the drop on The Cherokee Kid would be like stealing the rattles off a diamond back piece of lightning. The prairie looked black when seen from town, but on the trail, the starlight seemed too bright. Any fast movement could be seen for a hundred yards or more. Several deer and a small herd of antelope had passed by in front of him and made him jumpy.

Quiet hours in the saddle had him anxious to get this posse stint finished. What he had thought would be, at worst, a few days was now closing in to a month on the trail. His spread back in South Dakota was small enough for Henry, his brother, to handle for a few days, but Jake had already been gone too long. If he arrested Pinkney tonight, it would still be a couple of weeks until he got home. With the reward and pay, he'd still be lucky to break even. Dragging a prisoner and the wounded sheriff through the hostile territory was another bad highlight to look forward to. Ever since he had stood tall to answer the call of his hometown, his luck had gone off a black cliff and he'd been plunging faster all the time.

When the Civil War began, Jake, the eldest son of a South Carolina farmer, had stood tall to do his duty. He had marched off proudly, certain that the south would teach those northern pencil pushers what it meant to be facing a fighting man. The true horrors of war crashed hard against him at the first battle of Bull Run. While his fellow southerners were rejoicing over the resounding victory, he was seeing a war that could not be won without the loss of the nation. By the time he was wounded and captured at Chancellorsville, he knew the south was doomed. His parents had lost the farm in Sherman's march to the sea. He lost track of his family months before he was captured.

His first trip to the north was in a boxcar full of defeated, captured rebs. The North's POW prison was in Chicago. After serving in the Army of Northern Virginia, incarceration was a walk in the park. Precious food was simple but ample. The guards were easy going older men, glad they weren't being sent south to fight. Frequently, the gates would be left open and unguarded. Where could the rebs escape to? Few ever left. A thousand mile trip to rejoin a losing cause had little appeal. During his second week in Chicago, Jake had boosted a set of civilian clothes off a wash line and kept right on walking. Settling eight hundred miles to the west near Belle Fourche, he spent the years until the war ended, watching for the Army patrol sent to recapture him.

Letters sent to the farm's address in South Carolina were returned unanswered for several years. On the third Christmas, Henry, Jake's younger brother sent him a letter. He joined Jake in the springtime. No other family members survived.

Two hours into his ride, Jake saw a dim light off in the distance, ghostlike in its faint changing shape. As he approached, he realized it was merely the residual heat of the prairie reflecting the light that escaped the windows. Stopping several hundred yards off, he listened and watched. Tying his mount on the far side of the corral, he slowly climbed the steps to the cabin and drawing his sidearm, knocked gently on the door.

Anne

LUGUNEA ANNE HILDERBRANT stirred restlessly late into the night. By the small light still given off by her cook stove, she could see well enough to untangle herself from the arms of Jewel and Adam, who still slept soundly. They had joined her tonight, seeking comfort.

Standing and straightening her clothes, she looked at her two precious children. They were so young, so innocent. The long days with the tension they felt since the arrival of Dan and the death of their father was unseen to the casual eye, but obvious to her. They tired so rapidly now.

She was restless and alone. The absence of Dan worried her now as she had never experienced before. The path ahead seemed rocky and unsure. She was certain of Dan's abilities and loyalties, but the Sweets' ranch was huge. There were too many enemies for one man, even if that one man was Dan Pinkney. She was filled with a sick fear that she might be the cause of his death and perhaps the death of her children, all because of her stubborn refusal to leave this homestead. Could she bear to live in a place that could cost her everything?

A deep and unreasoning dread filled her, clutched at her chest, and she began to gather the things she needed to leave this place. She must get away while there was still time. They had so few possessions that she had packed quickly. They would move to a new place, where life would be better than staring into the uncertainty of existence here on the prairie. She could load everything onto the wagon and be safely away before first light. Just start moving west over the mountains, and Dan would find them. She couldn't bear the thought of losing him while trying to hold on to that which was indefensible.

Her dress brushed against a chair and the slight scrape caused Adam to move restlessly in his sleep. The sound and movement although slight, broke the grip of fear and she stood quietly as it drained from her.

Now, by the power of my God, she thought, this is my place, Adam and Jewel's place, and Dan's place too, if he could conquer the restless beast which lived within him. That part of him, which she had never understood, had caused him to move throuhout his life.

Angry at the weakness she had felt within her, she checked the load in Burt's old pistol, then rechecked the Winchester and her shotgun. She would be ready to face that which would surely come.

She heard a gentle knock on the door and threw her shawl over the pistol on the table, not wanting Dan to know that she'd been so fearful. Running to the door and throwing it open, her, "Oh Dan," was cut short by the appearance of a stranger with his gun drawn.

"Hello, Mrs. Hilderbrant, my name is Jake Andly. I'm here to arrest Dan Pinkney. Do you mind if I come in for a minute?"

Ambush

DAN RODE SOUTH from Dry Creek. The late afternoon sun was beginning to relent on its heat as he finally pulled his mount west. He felt the need to look over the southern foothills that formed the lower prominence giving the valley its distinctive V-shape. He had scouted the northern foothills that morning. Now he wanted to see what the territory to the south looked like. Without question, familiarity of the terrain could only be a help if a range war broke out.

The bluffs and swells of the mountain began less than ten miles out of town. There were no flowing rivers and the prairie around him was featureless. Finding nothing of significance, he turned his horse toward the homestead and followed the line of the foothills home.

Buzzard love, he thought, as he rode. Seems nothing but grief in this hand I've been dealt. There's not much but enemies in this land, all wanting to feed on my carcass. The careless time of endless freedom, the heady recklessness of his life, was gone forever. Anne and the children had given his life, from this marker onward, a richer depth and meaning. He was taking a giant step to the future.

An hour and a half later, with full dark almost on him, while his thoughts were centered on the warm cabin and hot coffee located a good eight miles ahead, his horse went on alert. Ears erect, head turned to the south, Dan, an experienced rider, knew there was something moving in the dark. Pausing for a moment, he searched for any clue. What had spooked his mount? He unfastened the leather strap holding his Sharps. It was probably just a deer, maybe a bear, better to be ready. He swung another twenty yards out into the prairie and kicked his mount up to a canter. An angry buzz slipped past, close to his head, followed immediately by the report of a rifle. Hardly hitting full stride, his horse stumbled and threw Dan against the saddle pommel. The roar of rifle fire seemed to surround him, and he swung down low off to the horse's left side to shield himself. He felt blood spraying from the animal's neck and he covered the wound with his hand, trying to hold it tight enough to stop the blood flow. Instinctively the animal's flight reaction threw him forward at full gallop. Less than fifty yards ahead, the animal began to fall. Dan snatched at his rifle, shook his feet loose from the stirrups, and fell off the right side of the dying animal. Luckily he had not been hit, but he had clearly felt three rounds shudder into his mount. He slowly fed a round into the Sharps .44 caliber and quietly seated the bullet. At times like this, a Winchester, with its rapid fire capacity, would be handy. Still Dan preferred the Sharps with its heavier bullet. The .30-.30 round from the Winchester could reflect off brush and small branches that the heavier bullet from the Sharps would tear right through and remain on course.

Looking over the edge of the ditch into the blackness of the hillside, he eased his rifle up to where it could be of use. Aiming at where his instincts directed that the first round had been fired, he waited, trying to remember the sequence of shots. The first had been fired on level with his horse, the second was higher up the hillside, and the third rifle shot sounded to be five to ten yards ahead of where the first shooter had fired. Dan believed the first ambusher would usually be the most anxious, and he kept the rifle pointed in his general area. His horse jerked and kicked out in its death throes, and Dan saw the muzzle flash in the dark. Pulling in on the sound and with the vision of the man still burning on his retinas from the fast flash of the muzzle, Dan gently caressed the trigger. The huge buffalo gun roared into the night and a man's scream filled the quiet.

Dan rolled to his right, came to his feet and ran to his fallen horse. He had just slid behind it, when two rounds ripped the ditch up where he had lain seconds before. That helps clear up that mystery, he though. There are at least two more skunks out there, and one man close to death if not already there. Anyone hit by the .44 caliber round, anywhere on his body, was instantly in serious condition.

Lying next to his horse for cover, Dan slowly fed another round into the chamber. He laid it gently up on the body of the animal, aiming it somewhere near where he thought the third man lie. Still the quiet beat down hard on them, a bother to hunter and hunted. Each was desperate to locate the other. The faintness of the starlight was enough to give away a big movement, but slow movements were practically undetectable by the human eye in the darkness. Dan watched for what seemed hours, and could pick out no movement. Holding his breath, he could hear no sound over the beating of his heart. "These are cowboys," he thought, "How good can they be?" Still, he could find nothing to reveal their presence.

"All right," he thought, "we can do it the hard way. They must a forgotten, I'm a Cherokee Indian. I move invisible in the night. My childhood was spent at play preparing for this night." Dan knew he couldn't wait past first light, or they would have him pinned down and would kill him in the crossfire.

He unbuckled his belt and removed his jacket, slipped the boots off his feet. He'd lived barefoot most of his life and now would need the sensitivity of his feet to keep from making any noise on the hillside. He pulled his knife from his boot and picked up one pistol, checked the rounds to make sure it was loaded, and began to crawl slowly around the horse to the hillside. He used the crawl developed by the southwestern Indian tribes that was almost undetectable in fading light or darkness. They were the first guerrilla warriors and he was one of the best. His arms were extended before him, and he would rise up on his toes and pull himself forward a foot, then repeat. It was brutally slow, but he reached the hillside without drawing fire. He stopped frequently to watch and listen. He worked his way into the brush, feeling each step with his feet before putting his weight down. He moved a full five yards up the hillside, then turned and began moving east toward his prey. Unless the ambushers had been trying to work their way west, he should be in range of the first bushwhacker in several more yards.

Leaning against a tree, both feet planted solidly on the earth, Dan closed his eyes, held his breath, and listened. The man was there. His breathing was discernable over the ambient night noises. Locating him by sound, Dan focused his eyes to the right. Gradually the form of the ambusher came into focus. The man was sitting, with his rifle balanced on his knees, looking out over the prairie. Suddenly, the wounded man moaned in the night, somewhere far to the east of where Dan now stood. The hill sitter turned his head slightly to look over in the direction of the man. By the time he looked back out over the prairie, Dan had taken four rapid steps, and with his right hand thrust his knife. The blade had entered the back of his neck and had sliced through the top of his spine and ripped well up into his brain. There was no sound or visible movement, it happened too fast for the man to react. One second, he was a hunter, now he was rag doll body lying on the hillside.

Dan laid him quietly on the forest floor and carefully holding the man's Winchester, began to move slowly back up the hill. He knew there was at least one other man, but forced himself to search for two or more. His memory of the first shot fired at him seemed to be much higher than the fire received from the other two shooters. He was sure the second shooter was the man he had killed with the buffalo gun. Now, he began to climb the hillside until he neared the ridgeline. Crawling slowly to the east, listening, watching carefully in the dark, he could find no sign of the man. Sitting against a thick tree trunk, watching the field of fire, trying to determine where he would have fired from, he located where he believed the third ambusher lie hidden. Aiming the Winchester at the suspicious patch of black, he waited. Patience on a hunt is a virtue. In a gunfight such as this, it can be a life saver. First to reveal his position would be the first to die.

The noise was very light. Dan heard it but could not pinpoint it. He could focus it down to a general ten yard area, but the source of the noise was too hidden to begin firing at. He tried to crawl closer, but a stone bluff was right beneath him and it allowed no easy passage. Working around the cliff was prevented by a large patch of black thorny brush. Now the hard decision, should he fire and end this quickly, knowing that Anne would be waiting nervously for him at home, or should he wait until the clear shot was revealed. Starting to slowly squeeze the trigger, a slight noise drifted to him. Something like a boot scraping against a tree trunk, as if a man was gripping tightly, had generated a small sound. Dan looked upward at the tree near him and saw a moving shape coming down the tree. The man was still twenty feet off the ground when the bullet took off the top of his skull. The fall would have killed him if the bullet hadn't. Dan rolled rapidly to his right and lay motionless for twenty minutes. He was beginning to see the sky lightening in the east. Hearing and seeing no others, he rose and returned to the body of his horse. Pulled on his boots, jacket, and gun belt, he went back to the hillside and dragged the bodies down to the prairie.

A short search revealed the horses tied to a small sapling near the man in the tree. One of the men now lying lifeless was Blondie. "He came for revenge," thought Dan. The man killed by the buffalo gun was the blond man's friend when Dan had caught them over near the creek. The third man was unknown. The horses were all Slash S brands.

Maybe Sweets had decided it was time for war, and decided to let the two men have revenge for the humiliation at the creek. It had been a carefully planned ambush and would have probably worked if he had ridden home while it was still light enough. The darkness had saved him. Dan was going to have to brace Sweets and find out his intentions. He cut the saddles from two of the horses, and tied the three bodies onto those two animals. He resettled the third horse with his gear and rode back toward the cabin.

The morning sun had filled the valley with light by the time Dan approached the house. He stopped several hundred yards from the corral studying the horse tied to the far side of it. It wouldn't be a Slash S rider, they would have thought he was dead. It had to be the deputy from the posse, here to arrest him. The children and Anne would be in the cabin with him now. He sat quietly and watched for several minutes, playing out in his mind a scenario that would allow the safety of the kids.

Dismounting, he took the bridles off the two horses that carried the bodies, and turned the animals loose. They stood patiently for a few minutes, then began to graze and move away to the east. Dan remounted and rode up to tie his horse next to the deputy's. He unfastened his gun belt and left the weapons hanging over the pommel of the saddle, walked slowly to the door and knocked.

Anne opened the door, "Run Dan, run, it's the deputy, he's come to arrest you."

"It's okay, Anne," he said. "We knew they were coming." Entering the cabin, he left the door open wide, and took a seat at the table.

"Good morning, kids, anyone got a hug for me?" They both ran to greet him. "Everything is okay here, so can you two play outside while your mom and I talk to this man for a minute?"

Jake stepped out from behind the door where he had been standing out of sight. His pistol was out and he had it casually pointed at Dan's chest.

Dan looked at him with an air of unconcern. "Ya caught me, officer. I'm Dan Pinkney, probably better known to you as The Cherokee Kid. What's your name, so at least I'll know what to call you?"

"Jake Andly, Deputy Jake Andly."

"Well Deputy Andly, I'm not armed. Mrs. Hilderbrant and the children pose no threat to you, so if you would uncock that cannon of yours, I'd be grateful."

Jake pulled a chair away from the table and sat near the cabin wall, away from the door. He uncocked his pistol, but still held it in his hand.

"Deputy Andly, I give you my word that I'll not try to escape. I will ride away from here peaceably as long as you don't hurt the woman or her kids. In the meantime, this lady has got to feed her children. Perhaps we can persuade her to fix a plate for us, and maybe a large steaming cup of coffee. I imagine your night has been as long and busy as mine, and a little coffee might make the world a better place."

"Pinkney, I have been trailing you for nigh on to three weeks, and I'm not letting you slip out of my grip now."

"I just promised you I would go with you Jake, but it's your choice, because I'm going to have breakfast now and a cup of coffee whether you do or don't. I happen to know this lady is an excellent cook, and I'm thinking grub after here will be on the middlin side. After I eat, I'll ride with you if you still wish. If that's unacceptable to you, just shoot me now, and drag me on out. I might smell pretty bad before you get me back to South Dakota that way though. Seems a mite easier if you do it my way, but you being a southern gentleman and all, you might not be trusting a shifty black man. You do it your own way." Dan smiled at him, held his hands up, "I'm reaching into my shirt for my makings. The guns are all out there hanging on my saddle horn. My horse is tied up next to yours."

Dan pulled out the brown papers and spread some loose tobacco onto one sheet of it. He rolled and lit a smoke, leaving the makings on the table, and motioning to Jake to help himself if he wanted. Mrs. Hilderbrant set down two steaming cups of coffee, one in front of Dan and one where Jake's place would be if he came back to the table.

"You let a black man eat at your table, ma'am?" asked Jake.

"That black man, as you call him, is, first of all, a man. His name is Dan Pinkney, as you should know. And yes, Dan Pinkney is, and always will be, welcome at my table. It's him as feeds my children and it's him as is helping me hold on to my homestead when the white ranchers are trying to force me out. The white people in town are too busy wringing their hands and quivering in fear of the Slash S to help me."

She dished up the food for the two children and sent them out onto the porch to eat this morning. She put a plate in front of Dan, and one in Jake's place, and sat down to eat her own.

Watching them for a minute, the smell of the food overcame his caution. He had not been prepared for the man's attitude after being captured. "You gave me your word, right?"

"That's right, I'll go with you after I finish my coffee."

Jake pulled up his chair, picked up his spoon, and by the time he got the first bite of food to his mouth, Anne had pulled her pistol out from beneath the shawl and had it cocked and pointed at Jake's head. "Run, Dan," she said, "don't let them take you because of me. Wherever you go, me and the kids will find you."

"That's okay, Anne, I gave this man my word. Now put that hog leg away and let's enjoy this wonderful meal you made."

"Dan, listen to me. This is a lawman, more tin star than real man. He's got no heart, only a purpose. Giving your word to him don't mean spit."

"But it means everything to me, Anne. Please put the gun away. Then we can enjoy this wonderful food and can talk. At worst, I'll be gone a couple of weeks and then I'll be back."

Anne stood, took the pistol back to her pantry and left it on a shelf, then returned to the table. "Shoulda killed him, just shoulda killed him," she murmured as she finished up her plate.

When Mrs. Hilderbrant had cleared the table, Dan with coffee cup in hand, turned to Jake Andly.

"What do you hope to get from my capture, deputy?" he asked.

"I'm taking you back because that's what I swore I would do."

"That's honorable of you, but I suspect my having a reward on my head was more of an incentive, if not for you, for your sheriff."

"I should get half the reward, and they'll pay me a couple of bucks a day to be on this posse. As long as I'm a deputy of Belle Fourche, I am obliged to carry out my job."

"I'm afraid you might have somewhat of a problem coming that you don't even suspect. A federal marshal has cancelled that reward poster. You can wire Marshal Earp in Dodge City to verify what I'm saying, but from the look on your face, I suspect you know I'm telling the truth. Sheriff MacCaffee, in Dry Creek, would verify it also."

"You are still wanted in South Dakota for the bank robbery charge. The bank guard died, which makes it a capital crime. You could end up swinging."

"That's the second thing you truly have no clue about, and it's just good luck for you that you didn't capture me earlier."

"What the hell you talking about?"

"That so called bank robbery. I wasn't involved in it at all. If you get me back, the bank president and the livery stableman will both testify that I wasn't involved. Now they might hang me anyways cause they don't like blacks much in South Dakota, but the fact still remains, that I wasn't involved in the bank robbery."

"Why did you run if you weren't involved?"

"Easy answer. The sheriff saw me, pointed me out, and shouted to everyone that I was involved. They were all shouting at me so I fled. What puzzled me for a long time, is why did the sheriff go out of his way to involve me? I think that answer is bad news for you. I think you were tricked into taking this job, and it was a job you were never meant to complete."

"So you're telling me this whole posse bit was a set up?"

"It was. You followed a man you trusted, but he had no good intentions for you. I think you were meant to be dead by now. Could be you should start thinking a little yourself instead of just follow-ing the sheriff's directions. If you could look back at the sheriff's desk, I'm pretty certain there is a poster of me lying near the top of his pile. When he saw me, he saw a chance to make an easy five hundred. He picked a posse that he knew would not ride for more than one or two days. I'm unsure how you ended up on the posse, but he either didn't expect you to go, or believed you wouldn't last more than one day. What I'm sure of is that if you had captured me, you wouldn't have made it back to collect any part of the reward. I would have ridden back draped over a saddle, and you would be lying somewhere out on the prairie with a bullet in your back. So what do you think of my little take so carefully laid out by your sheriff so far?"

"Why did Earp dismiss the reward poster?"

"Cause the man I killed was drawing on me. It was a fair fight. People of Deadwood knew the man, not me, so I was judged guilty. It was a foolish charge without merit."

"Dan, I hope you don't mind if I call you Dan, let's pull these chairs out on the porch for a few minutes. I feel like a cigar and fresh breeze. I gotta work some of this through."

Sitting on the porch, Jake offered Dan a cigar. They both lit up, puffed enjoyably for a minute, watching the kids play in the front yard.

"My brother had just joined me, there was no way Steel would have known I could go on with the posse. He couldn't have known my brother would be there to watch my place."

"You got me stuck in a hard place," said Jake. "Trouble I've got is that I was suspecting the sheriff before you told me the story. Something is there in the sheriff that has just never rang true. But now I'm stuck with nothing but hard choices. My spread in South Dakota wasn't making enough for my brother and me to survive on as it is. That's why I part-timed as a lawman."

"I ain't much on long term answers for you Jake, but for the short course, I have a few suggestions." Jake and Anne both looked at him.

"Just a minute, Jake," Dan said. "Our horses are standing out there in the sun. Since we're not using them for a little time now, I'll go put them in the corral, let them get a little water and shade."

"Hey Adam," he called, "want to come and help me?"

Adam ran down to the corral behind Dan. After Dan had taken off their saddles, Adam led them into the corral and began rubbing them down. "You're doing a good job of that, Adam. I'm real proud of you," said Dan.

He carried both saddles up to the porch and stored them in shade. He said, "I hate to see dumb animals suffering in the heat. Now, about this morning, I sent three dead bodies back to the Slash S right before I walked in here. They tried to ambush me last night, and it took most of the night for me to find and kill them. Don't know what response Sweets or Fiori will have, but I'm betting it won't be a tea party with cake. I was going to wait for them on the front porch and have Mrs. Hilderbrant and the kids inside the cabin. Seems to me that one more man with a rifle standing by that corral post there," he pointed to the stout corner pole, "would certainly be an additional deterrent to any hostile gunfire. I realize this is not your concern, but I'm suspecting you don't want to see this lady get driven out of her home. You're too much man to turn your back on them."

"I will help. I can't turn my back on them either. But you're still my prisoner, agreed?"

"Jake, I am still your prisoner, but I need to talk to Mrs. Hilderbrant for a few minutes. Would you excuse us for a few minutes?"

Jake walked down to the corral and started to fill the trough with water. He also forked down hay for the animals to feed. He stood quietly in the shade watching them eat. It was hard for him to not trust a man that was laying his life out to help a woman in need. A bad man would not have worried about the mounts being tied out in the sun. His mind was torn between duty and honor.

Dan turned to Anne. "What do you think of him?" he asked her.

"He seems okay for a lawman. I don't want you to ride off with him. So I have fear also."

"I have a plan for the homestead and making it secure, but I'm going to need another man who is a hard worker and knows how to handle a gun. We need money for hay and we'll probably have to put up a fence. He's the most reliable man I've run into out here. My suggestion to you is that we hire him, then there would be room for him and his brother to build their own place.

"First things first, I love you and I would like to be married to you and spend my life with you. Don't give me an answer yet. Let me lay out the full plan.

"I checked the deed to your homestead when I was in town. This was considered wasteland at the time, so your property line is about two hundred yards south of here, and it extends from the top of the foothills on both sides reaching back to the mountains. You actually own quite a huge chunk of land.

"My plan is that you and I hitch up the wagon and go talk to the Sweets' ranch and the other two ranches. Let's see if we can handle this all peaceably. It will be dangerous, but you being the owner must be there. My word would carry no weight.

"That rain that fell this morning might be the end of the drought. Could be they'll all be in a great mood."

"My answer is yes. I will marry you. I will go with you anywhere, and I have complete faith in your plan. My life, as I see it, didn't exist until you rode down off that hill. It will end when one of us dies, and I will go through any danger to keep us together. You make the plans, I am totally with you," said Anne.

"I love you, I will forever. In two weeks, we will have secured our place in the valley forever, or we will have been forced out. With a woman like you by my side, I can move heaven or hell," said Dan, taking Anne in his arms and kissing her.

Dan walked out to where Jake was standing near the well. "Feel like relaxing with us today? I have some suggestions for you."

Jake looked up at the mountain, then back at Dan. "I do. Got a bunch of crap to run through my brain. There's a path laid out for me, just have to figure out where it goes."

"Let's hook up the wagon," said Dan. "We'll go over to the stream for a picnic and maybe go swimming."

Less than an hour later, with a picnic basket packed up, they were on their way over to the small stream on the far side of the valley. Dan unhitched the team and let them graze while Anne and the kids laid out the blanket with the food basket set on it. Jake built a campfire and started a pot of water for coffee. The deep shade with cool running water was perfect. Jake was soon sitting against a tree, nodding off after the long night.

"Let's go swimming," shouted Dan, and taking off his boots waded out in the shallow creek.

"Be careful, Dan, they've never been swimming before."

"Come on kids, last one in is a flop eared dog."

They both took off their shoes, but hesitated at the edge of the stream, sticking one foot out to test the water. Finally Jewel took the step out and walked to where Dan was standing. "Ooh it's so cold," she said, and Adam, no longer able to resist, not wanting to appear afraid, waded out to join them. Dan pulled off his shirt and lay down in the moving water. He began splashing the kids, and soon pulled them down too. Splashing and playing tag, they had a wonderful afternoon. The best time they could remember. The water and the breeze tired them quickly, and they came ashore for the lunch packed up by their mom. Having eaten a little, soon Jewel and Adam were sound asleep on the blanket.

"They are the best tykes ever," said Dan.

"And this might be their favorite day of all," said Anne. "I'm heading up stream a ways to take a bath," she showed him a bar of soap.

Dan nudged Jake's foot. "Hey, let's talk a little while everyone is busy. See if we can work out a few things."

Jake walked out into the stream and washed his face, poured a hot cup of coffee, and sat down near Dan. "Seems like years since I had such a relaxing day."

"This is paradise found. I want to stay here forever," said Dan. "Problem we got, is trouble in this valley will soon boil over. I'm going to try to end everything without violence, but there are hot-heads everywhere.

"Look around you. Everything you see is Mrs. Hilderbrant's. It's too big for just her and me to run. I'd like to enroll you as a partner. Your brother is more than welcome to come out and stay with you. This would be a flat out partnership. After making sure the kids and Anne eat, everything else would be split down the middle. That said, I gotta tell you I got no money right now, got lots of ideas but no money. I think between the two of us, we can make a go of it. What I'm offering is a handshake agreement on a lot of trouble and hard work. That will last just as long as both of us want it. There is lots of room for you to build your own place. Whatcha think?"

"Dan, you know I've come to trust you and I like the family, great kids. And I certainly wouldn't mind leaving South Dakota in the dust. What I see you got though is not much but a dozen horses, a small garden, and a ton of enemies. Now you tell me you have no money. It's one helluva offer."

"Sound like it will be too hard for you?" asked Dan.

"Don't see an upside to this," said Jake.

"Wouldn't need a partner if it was going to be easy," said Dan.

"Any chance you're going to tell me your plans before I jump in?"

"Not really. I can promise you a lot of hard work and sweat," said Dan.

Jake pulled out his makings and shook a paper loose. He slowly built himself a smoke, offered the package to Dan who took it and started working on his own. Jake lit one, and stepped back out of the shade into the sunlight prairie. He saw himself standing at the cross-road of his life right now. This decision would change everything. He liked Anne and Dan, but had known them less than a day. Still, he'd known the sheriff better than a year and hadn't recognized him as a lying, cheating, back shooting bastard. So many of his decisions had been wrong, but in the changing of the societies around him, he'd always acted as he felt he must. Nothing remains stagnant, but he needed to maintain his balance. The ranch in South Dakota was a bust, but starting with nothing but a new partner? He walked back to Dan. "Tell me just a bit more."

"This country has been gripped by a drought for the last five years. The ranchers have let their cattle drift as they no longer had as many hands to control them. The hillsides and upper meadows got a lot of old mossy horns that have been squeezing out calves for all that time. I figure we could start rounding them up and selling the unbranded cattle back to the ranchers, or if we can get enough, say a hundred or two, we could drive them down to the fort to sell. Army is always looking for good beef. That's my big plan for starter money. Like I say, it'd all be fifty-fifty. Maybe we could start our own herd with a new brand. We got enough water and grass. Couple of years, maybe we could buy out one of the ranches. Hard cash goes a long way in tough times.

"One more thing you gotta know. I plan on getting married to Anne. You'll have a black partner married to a white woman and free access to all the bias crap that will come with it. You've been in town long enough to see some of the hate. Don't expect that to die off too fast."

"Sure you can't find one more black cloud to throw up?"

Anne came back into camp with streaming wet hair and looking fresh as morning dew.

"If it's alright with Anne, and you both agree to the terms, I'm with you, but it's gotta be me and my brother."

"Welcome aboard Jake," said Anne.

"I had a feeling about you from the jump. Tomorrow is the start. It'll be a long day, but by the time the sky turns dark, we'll probably know which way our coin is going to fall," said Dan.

Sweets' Response

DAN, IN THE cooler shadow of the cabin, stripped to his waist, and was splitting firewood with Adam and Ruff by his side, when the alert call came from Jake. He's been working with the horses in the corral. He saw the dust ball rising several miles down the valley. "Dan," he called, "I think they's coming. Better get the tykers in the cabin and lock the door. Annie, keep your shotgun loaded just in case." Pinkney and Andly checked their loads. Dan put on his shirt and removed his gloves. He sat on the front porch as the six men rode into the front yard. Less than twenty feet from him they pulled up. The only man Pinkney recognized was Al Fiori.

Fiori spoke directly to Dan, "Thought I told you to keep riding, saddle bum."

Dan stood and drew both pistols, catching the riders off guard. He cocked both pistols. One he pointed at Fiori, the other was just aimed a little off to the left. "Should probably tell you here and now that I never did give a fresh cow-flop for what you told me. I'm here now and here I'll stay. Now iffin you want to force the action, two of you will go down fast. After that, it'll be a coin toss. But I suspect that shotgun looking at you out of that port will take out at least one more of you. The Winchester at the corner of the corral might make you a think a little before doing something rash.

"Now you rode up uninvited and unfriendly. Best be thinking of how much you're getting paid to risk your life trying to run off a poor widow and two little kids. Is it going to be enough to die for?"

The Kid had his eye on the rider to the far left of the line. He was a nervous, tousle haired lad with a wild look in his eye. He was the one who would cause the trouble, Dan was sure of it.

Pointing one pistol directly at him, Dan said, "You on the left, get off that piebald. Get off it right now, or I'll blow you off it." The nervous lad looked over at Fiori and then back at Dan. Aiming directly at him now, Dan began to count, "One, Two." The man dismounted and stood by his horse. "Now you," he pointed the pistol at the next man in line, "get off that hoss." He slid right off. Soon, all six men were afoot and looking at him. Dan fired both of his pistols over the men's heads and the horses took off at a run.

"I suspect them spindly legged pieces of crow bait won't stop running until they see home range. Now Mr. Fiori, let's us have a little palaver here. I talk best when the other guy is unarmed. So why don't you undo that gun belt and let it drop?" Fiori looked at him with cold hate. "Long as you got your hand down there, maybe you want to give it a try. Won't put me off none at all. Be a little hard for these men to drag your carcass back is all."

Fiori dropped his belt. One after another dropped their guns after Fiori folded. Dan walked five feet toward the men. "Back up you sleazy scum suckers, back up."

All six moved back a good ten feet. "Now, get them boots off."

"Jesus mister, you can't expect us to walk ten miles without our boots."

"I don't expect a thing of you, but at the count of three, I'm putting a round through any boot still on a man. One, two." Most of the men had their boots off or were working on them.

"Now here's the thing, you want your guns or boots back, just come on back any time you want. Next time, I might not be in a good mood and I suspect there will be a lot more gun smoke filling the air.

Iffin you lads ain't smart enough to figure out how things stand now, I don't see you getting smart enough to avoid an early death anyway."

Dan tied the men's hands behind their backs, while Jake hitched the wagon up.

"Now you six men is probably going to be working at them knots, and I can't say as I blame you. Couple of things you might want to consider, I'll be checking them bindings every once in a while. Every one untied or loose will result in that man walking the rest of the way to the Sweets' ranch. You stay quiet and I will let you go unharmed when we get there."

The tousle haired kid pulled and struggled against the ropes. "You ain't taking me back bound up like a calf to be branded," he shouted.

Dan pulled his .44 Colt and whacked him on the head. "Here you go kid. You might as well sleep some of the way back. Now the rest of you, get on that wagon, and carry that guy on too. See, when you bring stupid people, you gotta work more." He climbed into the wagon seat next to Anne and slapping the reins against the horses' backs, began the ride to the Sweets' Ranch.

A gentle rain had begun to fall, cooling off the prairie and soaking Anne's bonnet. Dan kept checking the cowboys' binds, but the only one who had worked the bindings off was Fiore.

Dan pulled him from the wagon. Fiori let himself be pulled from the wagon, then swung a hard right at Pinkney. Dan ducked Al's swing and smashed the man's nose with a right of his own. Pinkney let Fiori walk the rest of the way, while they continued on.

By late morning, Dan tied the team up at Sweets' hitching post, and helped Anne step down.

Looking out over the prairie, he could see the figure of Fiori, limping along slowly in bare feet. He could feel the hate emanating from the distant figure. The showdown with him was coming. It would not be long. Dan turned to the wagon and pulling the men out, removed their bindings. They looked at him with cold hateful eyes, but knew there would be no retaliation here. Barefooted and gunless, they walked off toward the bunkhouse.

Dan took Anne's hand. "Nothing will happen here, today. Just speak your mind to them, as one neighbor to another." Together they walked up the porch steps and Dan knocked gently on the door.

Elva answered the door.

Mrs. Hilderbrant introduced herself and Dan and handed Elva a cornmeal loaf she had baked that morning.

"Welcome, welcome to our house, neighbors. Let me call Candras. He'll want to meet and talk to you also. Here, take a seat and make yourself comfortable while I put on a pot for tea, or would you prefer coffee?" she asked.

"Tea sounds wonderful," said Anne.

Dan removed his hat, and unfastened his gun belt. He hung it on the hooks by the front door, and remained standing until Candras came into the room.

"Hard to believe you two would come calling here," he huffed in a gruff tone.

Dan walked over and extended his right hand. "Mr. Sweets, my name is Dan Pinkney. I want to introduce you to my employer, Mrs. Hilderbrant. Lugunea Anne Hilderbrant."

Caught off guard in an awkward situation, Candras shook Dan's hand, then walking over to Anne, said, "I'm pleased to meet you. Now tell me, what on earth would bring you to my ranch? Especially after sending three of my men back draped over their horses. "

Dan spoke directly to the old man. "I'm afraid that was unavoidable. Just unfortunate they worked for you. I was ambushed late last night and figure they's highwaymen trying to rob me. I have not laid their actions at your door. I thought you should know what happened so you wouldn't think I was out hunting your men. Should you want verification, I can take you to the site. My horse with at least three of their bullets in it is still laying there. Since they killed my horse, I confiscated theirs. What wages they had coming can be used to pay for the animal I took."

"So here you sit in my house, unarmed, giving me this line of who-struck-John. That horse has a Slash S brand. It's mine."

"So are the bullets that killed my animal. I figure we best let it be, not get the law involved, but I will leave that up to you," said Dan.

"Mr. Sweets," said Anne, "we came to visit our neighbors, not to be defending ourselves. If we are unwelcome here, Mr. Pinkney and I will ride out."

Elva walked in with a tray, "You are welcome, Mrs. Hilderbrant. It is so nice to meet you. Candras," she said firmly," keep a civil tongue in your head. These are the first visitors we've had in two years. You will not spoil this afternoon for me with more talk of the ranch. Mrs. Hilderbrant, I hear you have two darling children. Please bring them with you next time you visit. The thought of hearing kids running through this house again fills me with joy."

"Please call me Anne. I will bring them next time, seems like neighbors should know each other. My kids are growing so fast, and I'm sure they would love to meet you. You are certainly welcome to come visit us on the homestead."

"How are their lessons coming along?" asked Elva.

"Not too good," said Anne. "The school teacher in town has gone, and I'm afraid I haven't started them on learning yet."

"I still have the primers and some of the books my children used. Would you like them for your kids?"

Elva and Anne talked about schooling, spinning, and cooking for almost an hour. "Easy to see the ladies enjoyed each other's company," thought Dan.

He sat down next to Candras, who had remained quiet while Elva talked.

Dan started the conversation. "We understand your need for water and do not wish to shut you off from the deeper streams of the valley."

"That's generous of you. Are you saying we can run our cattle up there?"

"Well, we are in a way. We can't have your cattle in our yard, tearing up our garden and crowding the corral. So here's what our proposition to you is. We need barbwire to keep the cattle away from the house. We'll put up a fence, a hundred and fifty yards from the far hills which would give them plenty of room to graze and get to the water, but at the same time, we'd keep the home-stead safe.

"We want you to provide the wire, and a couple of hands to help me erect the fence. Also, because I'll be spending my time erecting the fence, we want two ton of hay for the horses."

"Seems I'm the only one who gets stuck with the expense."

"You can certainly ask the other ranchers to contribute their share. Don't suppose they will. But hell, wire and hay will be chump change to you. Anyway, you are the only one who has the necessary funds."

"Let me go talk to Rasty, my cattle foreman, and get his thoughts. I'll be back in a minute," said Candras.

Sweets went out the door, followed by Dan. Trusting Sweets at this juncture would be stupid, Dan felt the need to observe the yard to make sure no one was gathering. He pulled out his tobacco sack, and licked himself a smoke while he waited. Candras walked to the barn and entered. True to his word, he was back in a few moments.

"What the hell was that about?" thought Dan.

"God knows I hate that barbwire, but the deal seems equitable. I'll send Rasty in to order it up tomorrow and we'll deliver it when it arrives," said Sweets.

Under ordinary circumstances, a handshake was the prevailing western code for trust. Dan wasn't sure that was true of Sweets, but he extended his hand.

Leaving the Slash S, they traveled east to the Robertson ranch. Better known as the Double Bar R, Clyde Robertson and his wife

Annetta had a much smaller place than the Sweets. Chickens scurried in front of the horses, and there were hogs wallowing in a mud hole.

Robertson had built a windmill which drew water from the deep well and pumped it into a series of water troughs stretching out for half a block from the well. Ingenious man, thought Dan. Best way I've seen to keep a small herd watered. After discussing their plan for water access, Robertson was very friendly. "That's a generous plan considering how badly you've been treated by the Slash S." He said he would be willing to purchase a few unbranded calves, especially if the rain continued.

"Don't let Sweets know what you're doing," said Robertson. "He believes every living piece of beef in the world belongs to him or was probably stolen from him at night."

With half the day gone, they went to Dry Creek for supplies. The coming weeks would be full of busy work and they wouldn't have time to return. Dan had enough funds held back to buy Anne a new dress and bonnet. She changed in the back of the store, then came out to model it for Dan.

"Anne, you look so beautiful. You did say yes to me, and if you're still willing, I think we oughta talk to the preacher man today."

"I doubt that they'll let it happen that quick, always seem papers to slow everything down, but if we can do it today, I'm all for it."

Caught up in the excitement of the afternoon, they stopped in to see Sheriff MacCaffee. "We're going over to the church to hitch up for good, we'd be in your debt if we could get you to join us at our nuptials."

"Probably ain't going to be as easy as all that, and I'm not wearing fancy clothes, but I'll sure come and be honored."

Dan left his guns and hat in the sheriff's office, brushed the dust off his clothes as best he could, and the small party went to the church.

The preacher, Jim Brandt, was an older man, thin and stooped with the weight of the years he carried. In his deep resonating voice, he turned to Dan first, "You sure you know what you're getting into? There's a bunch of people in town here who will be very much opposed to you marrying Mrs. Hilderbrant."

"I do know that," said Dan, "but this beauty next to me is worth a lot of trouble." Dan paid the three dollars, the preacher gave a nice talk, and they were legally hitched. Dan kissed the bride, and together they left the church.

There was a group of men standing in the street, as Dan and Anne walked down the steps. One man, backed by two other men, turned to face them. "I'm Sheriff Steel from Belle Fourche, I have a warrant for your arrest, Dan Pinkney."

Dan stopped at the bottom of the steps leading from the church. "Better go back inside for a minute, Anne."

She turned and hurried back into the building. Sheriff MacCaffee walked out in front of where Dan stood. "Let me see that warrant, Sheriff," he ordered. He took a few minutes to read the paper, then handed it back to Steel. "That warrant is not valid in Montana Territory. You are out of your jurisdiction and have no legal right to make an arrest. And you, Dave Vegas, and you too, Jim Bob," he said as he pointed at the men, "What the hell you doing out here?"

"Helping the sheriff make an arrest," said Vegas, while Jim Bob nodded his head.

"Get the hell out of here both of you. My job's hard enough without you dragging your sore assed selves into this. So get moving or I'll arrest all of you for being an irritant and ignorant."

Vegas and Jim Bob looked sheepishly at Steel, then turned and walked off to the bar. Neither would ever have the sand to be able to stare down MacCaffee, and retiring seemed better than jail. Steel looked at the men's backs with scorn. "You scared the hell out of those two. You don't scare me. You won't shoot me in the performance of

my job, and my job is to arrest Dan Pinkney for bank robbery and murder." His eyes were focused on Pinkney.

"I won't let you arrest him in town. Also, he's unarmed, would you
shoot down an unarmed man?"

"Wanted men should arm themselves. The warrant reads dead or
alive. His hand blurred toward his gun and he fired fast from the hip.
If he had gone slower, he might have hit Pinkney, but his bullet ran
way too high. Before he could re-aim and pull the trigger, Dan rolled
to his right, pulled his knife from his boot, and threw it at the sheriff.
The eleven inch knife was also thrown too fast. It ran low, not high,
and the blade buried itself into the sheriff's lower stomach. Clearly
not a deadly throw.

The shock registered in Steel's eyes even as he stepped back to
catch his balance from the force of the throw. Stepping forward, he
tried to raise his pistol, but Sheriff MacCaffee's sidearm roared and
Steel's chest exploded with blood. He looked down to see blood curling from a chest wound pouring down and over Dan's blade. A puzzled look came over his face as he tried to lift his weapon, then slowly
he fell face first into the dusty street.

"That's one asshole that won't be bothering you no more, Pinkney.
He sure had it in for you."

"Greed was his downfall. He didn't never speak to me. Just
wanted that reward money. Damn strange how five hundred dollars
can ruin a man's soul. He lost everything he had chasing it."

A crowd of men came boiling from the bar to watch the drama
unfolding in the streets. "Arrest that man, Sheriff," said Al Fiori, over
the buzz of the men. "It was a deliberate murder. That black dog
killed a white man who had no chance to defend himself."

"You still on the street in another minute, Fiori, I'm going to arrest
you. I am the one who killed that man, not Pinkney. You want to
falsely swear a crime out, I'll put you in the pokey for sixty days."

Fiori looked hate at the sheriff. "You are arguing against the
Slash S again. You're wrong to ignore so many witnesses, MacCaffee.

Should be thinking about who put you into office, or you won't be sheriff long."

"But I am right now. You want to try to change that? Think your boss wants you to go against me? You see me standing right here in front of you, and I ain't backing water. Make your move or walk away."

Fiori's face was livid. He knew he could kill the sheriff and a wild feeling fell on him hard as he fought to maintain control. Killing MacCaffee would feel so sweet, but he knew such an act would turn the townspeople against him. His legs trembled with the effort needed to not draw against the man. He turned away.

"Slash S," he called, "we ride back to the ranch." He turned and left with his men towing in his wake like water behind a boat.

"We'll be back. Never fear, you'll answer for actions soon when you're alone with me."

MacCaffee watched the Sweets' riders leave town. He directed a couple of the townsmen to take Steel's body over to the coffin maker. "Tell him it's a town burial. A plain box'll do just fine."

He turned to look at Dan and Anne. "Well Mr. and Mrs. Pinkney, sorry this happened on your special day. How about stopping at The Eatery and I'll buy dinner before you head out. I feel a little guilty for not chasing that skunk out of town last week. Feeling sorry about his leg, I guess."

"Dinner would be a kindness, Sheriff." Dan and Anne were still embracing at the bottom of the few wooden steps leading into the church.

"Here's your knife, Dan. Guess Steel won't be needing it anymore."

Dan cleaned his knife by plunging it into the earth several times, then replaced it in his boot. The newlyweds walked up the street together, people made way for them with the sheriff leading the way.

MacCaffee held the door for the couple and they entered to an almost full dining room. The owner, Widow Griffin, ran out to meet them at the door. "I won't let a black man eat in here," she said defiantly.

"Yes, you will," the sheriff replied, "and you'll do it graciously as they are my guests. Come over here and let me talk to you for a moment alone, Sadie Mae." The sheriff went over to a corner with her and spoke softly. "What we have today is an opportunity to bring this town together. It's been split too long. There has always been trouble between the ranchers and the townspeople, this is a couple who is standing up against the ranchers. We need them and we need them to be accepted by everyone. Your goodwill and kindness now will go a long way toward healing Dry Creek. Without them, this town will die before long. I'm saying please, help me tonight, I will be so grateful."

He turned to the dining room and said in a loud voice, "We're here to celebrate their marriage today and by God, Widow Griffin, you're going to be polite. We want only the best you have."

The widow had been facing the window, looking out on the street. As she turned, her face broke into a big smile. "You will both be most welcome to my place." There's a time for standing firm, but for a store owner in a small town, there's a time when you bow to the necessity of the moment. This was such a moment.

"Please come in, Mr. and Mrs. Pinkney. Will this table be acceptable?" she asked, seating them near the door. I'll be with you in a moment. She hurried through the crowded room to the kitchen and returned in a minute with a bottle of wine with four glasses. "Try this, it's one of my best wines." She poured all four glasses, and handed each a glass. She lifted her glass to them, "A toast to the lovely couple. May your union be strong and happy. May the days bless you more with each passing year, and may you return here frequently to remember the start of your lives together."

They drank with her.

"Thank you for the toast, ma'am. It was as sweet and true as you are," said Dan.

She smiled back with a wry smile, excused herself, and went to the kitchen.

Soon she arrived carrying three loaded plates, piled high with charred beef and potatoes. They ate hungrily, keeping their eyes to the business at hand.

The room was unusually quiet. The couple felt the tension. Finally, one older man and his wife walked up to the table and laid his hand on Dan's shoulder. "Congratulations, Mr. Pinkney. You picked a good one to get hitched to."

The heavy quiet mood broke, and many of the remaining people came to the table to wish them the best.

The Widow Griffin came in, carrying a large cake with a lit candle on it, high over her head. "We all need a piece of wedding cake. She began cutting pieces of the large chocolate cake and dishing them out carefully to the crowd."

The warmth of the towns' acceptance filled them with a warm glow as they began the long ride home. The night was clear covered gently with glow of a spectacular starlight display. The wine sang in Dan's veins. This was his life now. No regrets looking back. The woman riding next to him was the finest he had ever met. He looked at her with a smile. Her grace and beauty were breathtaking, yet it was the strength of her being that drew him to her.

She saw the way he was looking at her. "It was so sweet that she brought out the cake. The people accept us, Dan. And now here I am, riding to my home with my husband. The best man I've ever known. Oh Dan, I will never be able to tell you how wonderful it is that some-one wants and loves me." She snuggled up tight against him and kissed his cheek. "I don't remember this feeling ever, but tonight I'm happy."

Legal Entanglements

THE CHILDREN WERE still playing in the yard, while Dan and Jake were preparing to head out on their first cattle roundup. Sheriff MacCaffee and a stranger rode into their yard and dismounted.

"Good morning, Sheriff. How can I help you?" asked Dan.

"Is Mrs. Pinkney here?"

"Sure she is. Just a minute, I'll give her a call."

Anne walked out on the porch brushing her hair from her face. "Good morning, Sheriff MacCaffee."

"Good morning, Anne. I trust all is well with you. I'm not here in an official capacity, and this is unpleasant for me. I came along to introduce you to Marshal Jeters. He's a federal marshal."

The man walked forward and handed a sheaf of papers to Anne. "I'm Marshal Jared Jeters. I am here to serve eviction papers on you. Your ownership of this land has been challenged. They allege this land ceased to belong to you upon the death of Burt Hilderbrant. The eviction notice is under the laws of the Territory of Montana. You must leave this homestead immediately."

"Where can I go with my children? This was their father's place before his death."

"Since your ownership of the land is being challenged under federal jurisdiction, a place has been rented for you in Dry Creek while we wait for the hearing. I'm sorry ma'am, but you must take the possessions that are yours and vacate the premises immediately. The hearing is set before Judge Abernathy in nine days. The ownership of the land will be decided at that time."

"Damn sneaky way to steal our land," said Dan. "Who will keep marauders off the land until the decision is made?"

"That's my responsibility. Not a worry of yours," said Marshal Jeters. "I will remain here to protect the land."

"Oh Dan, what are we to do?"

We'll take you to a place in Dry Creek to stay until the hearing. This is a land grab attempt by Sweets is all. Jake and I will take the horses down and sell them to the Army. That will get us enough money to do battle in the court."

"No. No stock can be moved from the premises until the hearing."

"So the only thin g we can take is personal possessions and the horses that were not owned by Hilderbrant. Can we use the wagon to move Mrs. Pinkney and the children into town?"

"Certainly, I understand that you need transportation, but don't take it further than the town."

Sheriff MacCaffee was surprised by the people in town when the day came for the hearing. All three ranchers and their hands were crowded into town. If the decision was made against the woman, they wanted to be recognized as having rights to purchase the homestead. The townspeople were crowded in the front of the hearing office which had been set up in the now abandoned schoolhouse. There was not enough room to seat everyone that wanted to attend, so there was a lot of pushing and shoving, trying to be at the front of the herd.

Judge Abernathy, a short, older man that walked with a limp, came out of the hotel at eight o'clock that morning and entered The Eatery for breakfast. The sheriff walked by his side and stood near his table to maintain solitude for the judge. He appeared not to hear the talk of those around him.

"Sheriff MacCaffee, we will need at least two more trustworthy men to act as officers of the court. Will you locate two such individuals in town and meet me back here?"

"Don't like leaving you alone."

The judge reached under his jacket and pulled out a Navy Colt revolver. He parked it on his table next to his plate. "I'll be okay. But please try to hurry."

MacCaffee left the restaurant running the list of townspeople through his head. Seemed to him impossible to find someone who hadn't picked a side, but a reliable man would still stand under the pressure. His first choice was Vern the bartender, a tough, overweight man who was widely respected in the town. Few men challenged Vern. MacCaffee's second choice was the blacksmith, Carl Applen. Although he was not a gunhand, he was as brave a man as MacCaffee knew and would keep the peace inside the schoolhouse.

Both men were hesitant, but MacCaffee was able to persuade them both to at least talk to the judge.

"I want you to understand what I'm requiring of you. You will stand at the front of the room, to keep order nothing else." The judge continued eating while he talked but he had a presence which was undeniable. He looked both men in the eye as he talked. "When this hearing ends, I want to be alive. You watch for any guns or knives out and ready to let fly at me. You will not talk unless I direct a question at you. When the hearing is over, you have to get me safely back to the hotel. Do you understand?"

He swore both men in, and following the sheriff and followed by Vern and Curt, he left for the schoolhouse. The crowd melted before them and they safely made the courtroom. Once inside the building, he set out several law books, a slab of wood and a gavel. "Okay, let the people in, but let them in slowly. Try to keep the uproar down."

At precisely nine o'clock, the judge banged his gavel down. "All rise." After seating himself, he said looked out at the crowd, "Everyone be seated."

"Any unnecessary noise or commotion out there, and I will clear the courtroom. If you have any questions, keep them to yourselves. The only people who will be talking in here are people I address.

"Now then, would you please bring in the plaintiff and counsel?" MacCaffee exited the room, returning moments later leading Sweets and his lawyer, seating them before the bench to the judge's right hand.

"Would you please bring in the defendant?" Dan and Anne entered with their lawyer, a younger man who had set up office forty miles south of Dry Creek.

"Now, Counselor," the judge said, "what evidence do you possess that would show Mrs. Pinkney not to be the lawful owner of the homestead in question?"

"First, Your Honor, I wish to point out that Mrs. Pinkney is in commission of a felony and therefore has no standing before the court."

"What is the felony that you accuse Mrs. Pinkney of committing?"

"She is in a bi-racial marriage. An interracial marriage is illegal in the Montana Territory. Congressman King of Kentucky submitted the bill in 1851."

"Indeed he did. He submitted the same bill in 1856. Since he resubmitted the bill, it's a reasonable to surmise that the bill didn't pass. Therefore, I find she is in a legal marriage and has standing before the court."

"Now shall we get on with the business at hand? Do you possess any evidence that Mrs. Pinkney is not the lawful owner of the homestead in question?"

"If I can approach the bench, Your Honor," the man said as he stood and picked up a stack of papers.

"This document shows that Burt Hilderbrant purchased the land in question by himself. There is no mention made of a wife. It's dated May sixth, 1866. Our contention is that since it was purchased by Mr. Hilderbrant as a single man, his death voided the title to the homestead. Therefore, Mrs. Hilderbrant has no title to the land. As this is a Territory of the United States of America, state law does not apply. And the territorial laws of Montana do not address surviving wives' inheritance."

"An interesting point of law, Counselor. Anything else you wish to present?"

"Not at this time."

He turned to the Pinkneys and asked, "Is there anything you wish to present?"

Their lawyer took the marriage certificate and laid it before the judge.

Judge Abernathy looked it over carefully. This document show you were married to Mr. Hilderbrant in November of 1865, prior to the purchase of the land.

"Is there a reason your name is not on the deed?"

"Your Honor," said Anne, "Neither Mr. Hilderbrant or myself could read. We depended on the clerk at the land office to prepare it correctly. We believed everything was in order."

The judge, looking up, asked, "Does anyone know of a Will left by Mr. Hilderbrant?"

"No Will was found," said Anne. "Burt couldn't write and the only lawyer in town, the counselor over there," pointing at the opposition bench, "said he didn't write one. Still, knowing them skunks, they might have doctored one up."

"We know of no Will," the lawyer responded, standing to address the court.

"Well then," said the judge, "I suppose it's time for me to make a decision."

"It's true what the plaintiff alleges, that no inheritance rights have been spelled out exclusively for the Montana Territories. That being said, this is a United States Territory, the jurisdiction of which has rule. Therefore, after considering the arguments of presented, I find that community property has been established in other territories including both Arizona and California. I rule that Mrs. Pinkney was legally married to Burt Hilderbrant at the time of his death and therefore, she is legally entitled to one half of his property. By looking at the map of the homestead, Mrs. Pinkney owns all the property on the north half of a line dividing the homestead into two parts. That is the first part of my decision.

The second parcel of land, that land south of the dividing line, is now owned by Mr. Hilderbrant's closest relative, that person being Adam Hilderbrant. By legal precedent of the Lord Mansfield rule, he is declared to be Mr. Hilderbrant's legal son.

I give full power to Mrs. Pinkney to act on his behalf on any legal matters pertaining to the land until he reaches the age of eighteen, when he will be able to act on his own behalf.

"Mrs. Pinkney is required to report to the court yearly, on the well-being of Adam and the use of his inheritance."

The court had exploded into chaos by the townspeople, and the crowd ran from the room to spread the good word to the group still milling outside. "We won, we won, cattle is no longer king."

The judge hammered the gavel down, "Court dismissed." He turned to MacCaffee, Jake, and Vern. "Get me back to the hotel in one piece if you can."

The sheriff led the way, followed by Judge Abernathy, and backed-up by Jake and Vern. Their guns were loose in their holsters, and they pushed their way through the crowd.

Back at the hotel, MacCaffee said, "Maybe I better get your rig set up so you can leave?"

"No. I'll stay tonight and leave tomorrow after everyone realizes that my ruling will stand no matter what happens to me."

With the schoolhouse empty, Dan hugged Anne. "We won but it was spendy, and it cost us almost two weeks of work. We are going to owe the lawyer and the livery stable, but now we have the homestead for good. Thank God for honest, fearless judges."

Later that afternoon, after eating together at the cabin, Dan took Jake aside. "Trouble is coming. That was just the first shot fired."

The Attack

"JAKE, BURT BUILT himself a cozy little cabin here. It's solid and easy to defend. But the truth is the man didn't know crap about war or rabbits. There ain't but one way in and one way out. Even a stupid rabbit has an escape hole and that's what I want to fix today. I'm thinking the gun port in the rear should be enlarged."

Dan brought in the crosscut saw and with Jake on the outside, they cut through the log under the opening in two places, then bolted the pieces back in place. "This is a just-in-case improvement. I don't want to be blockaded in here."

"Feels a lot safer now, I agree. Hope we never have to use it," said Jake. I'm going to take a little break and relax." Jake felt the need for a little solitude. The last two weeks had taken a toll with the ownership of the land and the continuing threat of Sweets. Taking his Winchester, he climbed the hill behind the house and sitting quietly, leaned against a tree. He'd spent his youth hunting and playing in a forest. The wilderness with its growth and abounding life still nurtured his soul. He ran the past few days through his mind.

The quiet of the forest was relaxing and he was looking out over the prairie. A few birds hovered close to him searching for the insects that flew around from bush to bush. With his old life behind him now and word sent to his brother to sell the spread and come out to Dry Creek, this valley could be the paradise they had dreamed of since the death of his parents at the start of the Southern Rebellion. He would build a small cabin; plenty of land to start a new life. Good friends to back him. Even the mountain streams held promise. Maybe he could try a little panning for gold.

He watched Dan, playing a game with the children. They used a stick to bat a ball of fur from one side of the yard to the other. Their happy shouts were soothing in a basic way. Maybe he needed a wife and a couple of his own children. That could drive out the empty feeling inside him since the death of his parents and sisters in South Carolina.

What he knew now was that trouble was coming. He could feel the tension building. Still this was his life now and woe be unto those who tried to take it from him. Looking down from his aerie, he could see a rider approach the homestead.

Riding a sorrel gelding, a lone cowboy rode into the front yard and reined to a halt before Anne and Dan. The horse carried the Slash S brand. "Mr. Sweets has two wagons loaded with hay and wire, heading this way. He wants to know if your agreement still stands?"

"It stands," said Dan, looking east over the prairie, but seeing nothing.

"It'll be an hour or two, the wagons are heavy, and the recent rain slows everything down," said the rider, as he turned his mount, and rode back toward the wagons.

"Get ready," Dan called to Anne. "We got an hour or two before he gets here, and I got as much trust in Sweets' good will as I do in my pet rattlesnake. Make sure the weapons are loaded, and let's keep the tykers inside until we see that things are going as planned." Dan rechecked the loads in his pistols.

Soon they could see the faint movement of the rough parade coming their way slowly. Anne stood on her porch in the shade. Dan stood out in front of the porch.

Sweets rode in first, tipped his hat, "Morning Mrs. Pinkney. Dan," he acknowledged with a nod, "where would you like me to dump the wire? Imagine you want this hay down by the corral."

"Next to the corral will be good for both, Mr. Sweets." Figured I'd start with the wire over west first, so's you'd be able to let you cattle in sooner. Give me a week to get it all up. Want to ride over with me and see where I mean to put it?"

"No thanks, Mr. Pinkney, I trust your placement of the fence."

Candras went back to his wagons. Several of the men had already begun forking the hay into a stack by the corral. Four cowboys rode up, dismounted, and tethered their horses to the wire wagon. One of Sweets' men was tying his horse to the far corner of the corral. Appearing to have trouble, he was taking a long time. Dan began to walk toward him, when the man stepped back, leaped into his saddle, and raced his horse away to the east. At the same time, the wire wagon turned and began rolling east also. Puzzled, Dan watched the cowboy who was dragging a long rope behind him, then the line went taunt, a loud crack sounded, and the corner post of the corral was torn down. Half of the fence was torn away. The horses panicked, bunching and leaping against the far fence, crying out in fear. The jarring sound of gunfire filled the air. Dan felt a round pass close enough to him that he could feel the small puff of disturbed air. He saw that half the cowboys were firing at the horses, the rest were firing at him.

From the hill, Jake was firing his rifle at the gunmen gathered near the corral. The first attacker he shot at dropped to the ground, but the rest scattered quickly. He began running down the hill to help. The fierce buzz of lead came from behind him, and he wheeled to see ten more attackers riding over the crest of the hill. He ran faster, trying to get away from them. The three bullets he had left in the Winchester wouldn't turn ten men. Nearing the corner of the cabin, a round hit him in the back, and smashed him face first into the ground. He rolled over, trying to stand, scrambled for the cabin and more ammo.

Dan drew both pistols and began coolly to fire at any cowboy standing near him. He saw two crumple and drop. He could hear Anne firing her shotgun from the porch. He waved at her to go inside the cabin, and turned to help Jake, when a burly cowboy to Dan's left rushed at him, trying to knock him down. Dan whipped his left arm, still holding the pistol, at the man. The heavy colt smashed into the man's nose. His head snapped backward then rocked forward slowly as he fell to the ground. Dan turned to throw a quick round at Sweets, and jumping in the direction of the downed burly attacker, brought his foot down solidly on the man's neck, and was rewarded by the sound of the man's neck breaking.

Sweets was standing on the wagon firing his rifle as rapidly as he could, when Dan's .45 round smashed into him. Candras screamed and fell backward from the wagon. The rate of fire increased suddenly, and Dan looked back at the hillside to see the group of mounted men riding at them, with their rifles belching fire. Ignoring the cracking firestorm, Dan began running toward Jake, firing both pistols. To remain exposed meant certain death for both.

Jake's shoulder hung awkwardly and blood ran down his arm. Dan helped Jake to his feet, and they ran to the relative safety of the cabin. They flew through the door as Anne slammed and bolted it behind them. Anne returned to the front gun port and cranked out lead at any target still standing. The roar of the shotgun from the eastern port was Adam. The kick of the weapon was knocking him around, but he stayed at his post and continued firing.

Pinkney, miraculously not hurt, went to the western port to look out. Seeing little move, he returned to take Anne's Winchester.

"Stop Jake's bleeding if you can," he told her.

He snapped a quick shot at a cowboy dashing in Sweets' direction and was pleased to see the man's leg explode into blood, knocking him into the ground. He rolled once, then crawled onward. Lead was raining on the cabin, but the thick walls provided protection. Dan put another round solidly into the crawling man's body. He coughed once, then lay still as his life force drained onto the ground.

"How many you count, Jake?"

"Four on the wagons and another five mounted. Another ten riders came down the hill. Fiori was leading the bunch on the hill. I killed one who was down by the corral."

"I got three of them for sure, and put a round into Sweets. I probably wounded two more. Better figure we got another fifteen of them out there still healthy. They all needs killing. I got a growing hate that wants to kill bunches of 'em. You up to handling a rifle yet?"

"Yep, we together on that. I'm heading for the back port."

"Keep them back or they'll fire the cabin." Dan didn't say it, but he knew the Slash S would have to kill them all to get away with this attack. If they let Anne and the children live, every rider out there would be a hunted outlaw. An attack against women and children would mark them. They would be dead men if caught. This fight was to the death. In front of the cabin, Dan could see four men behind the overturned hay wagon; they were firing rapidly at the cabin. Sweets had to be behind the wagon. Didn't figure he'd still be standing. There were men behind the downed lean-to and still more behind the wood pile of uncut logs. They had set up a perimeter around the house and dug in well. They were all thirty to forty yards out and would be unable to start the cabin on fire until they could work their way closer. There were four dead horses in the corral; the others had been run off.

Anne had gone to help Adam with the shotgun, while Dan watched the front and western ports. No one was moving outside of the cabin.

"Hold up on your fire unless you have a target. We've burned a good hundred rounds already. We gotta save the ammo."

Dan walked over to Adam. "Nice job, big guy. I'm real proud of you." He took the big gun from Adam, stuck two more shells in it, and poked it out the western port. "Fire at anything you see standing or moving," Dan said.

Reloading the Winchester, he gave it to Anne. "Keep an eye on Adam if you can. That guns too big for him, but he's sticking it out like a trooper."

"Need ammo?" he asked Jake.

"Okay so far, still got twenty rounds left in the box."

Dan walked over to Jewel who was lying on the bed with her face in a pillow. Dan patted her on the back. "Don't be too afraid, I'm not going to let anything happen to you, sweetheart." He gave her a stick of hard candy, "Suck on this, and it'll keep your throat from being too dry."

He gave each of the others a sucker also, "Extra energy."

Dan took his buffalo rifle off the wall, chambered a round, and took a long look at the wagon out front. The floor of the wagon was a thin layer of wood, supported by crossbeams every four feet. He watched the men hidden behind the wagon. They would lean over the edge, fire a round, and duck down behind the wagon again. Watching only the man at the front of the wagon, he began to count how long it took for him to complete the cycle. When he believed he had the timing right and a good mental picture of the man in his mind, Dan aimed at where the man's head was while firing, then pulled down about a foot and a half, and waited. The man fired, ducked back, and Dan counted to three and squeezed the trigger. Small chunks of wood blasted outward, and a hat went spiraling backward, twisting wildly, throwing pieces of skull and meat in all directions. One less enemy.

He put two more rounds into the wagon, but saw nothing else.

"Switch with me, Anne."

She came to the front while he moved to the eastern port. Dan loaded another shell in the big gun. The cowboys had dug in good. He could see little. The horses were out there, tethered to a broken corral section. The wire wagon had dragged it a good four hundred yards out. Targets of opportunity. Dan estimated the wind drag, slowly tightened his grip on the trigger, and the huge rifle leaped in his hands. The front horse screamed and went down kicking, panicking the other animals which pulled and jerked at their tethers. Two pulled free and ran off, the others pulled at the section of fencing, dragging it toward the Sweets' ranch.

"That'll put a limit on their ammo supply," thought Dan.

Horse screams filled the afternoon air. Finally one of the cowboys, unable to bear the sound, shot and killed the wounded animal. After the barrage, quiet fell hard on the cabin. The Slash S had meant to crush them rapidly, but now they were forced to rethink their attack. The best plan now was to wait for night, and burn the cabin down. In the dark they could easily close in on the cabin.

"Let's have a little lunch while we're waiting," said Jake, as he stood and stretched. "Can't believe that guy got me, just carelessness on my part. I shoulda been ready and watching closer."

"Ya, well they were ready and had their guns out while we watched the corral go down. That sorry son of a red eared dog Sweets bit into a bitter biscuit with this attack."

"We'll be leaving at dusk. We don't want to leave anything for them, so what we don't eat or shoot, we carry. Get the children dressed in their darkest clothes. You can use the ash from the fire to make sure nothing white is showing. Gotta a feeling they'll be rushing the house right at dark, so we don't want to be here."

"We'll be going out the back, but we'll have to move fast to evade them sorry bastards. Think you'll be strong enough to keep up, Jake?"

"Hell lad, you got no worries with me. They picked the wrong place to attack. Probably didn't no one tell 'em I was a partner with you. They'll all pay for this. I've fought harder battles against longer odds with less cover. I'm way too tough for these skunks."

"I'm thinking this buffalo gun is too heavy to carry. I plan on burning up some of this ammo for it. Really hate to lose it. It's been a grand piece. Let me see if we can get someone to rabbit," said Dan.

He fed a round into the chamber, aimed at the top timber on the woodpile. He hit the log dead center. It rocked it up on the wood behind it, then settled back where it had been. A deep hole was scored into the log. His second round smashed into the same place on the timber, tearing wood from the previous hole. The log rolled up again, but bent in the middle and didn't roll back. With his third round, Dan aimed at the far right end of the timber, almost torn in half, lifted the right side of the log, and the log leaned over the edge of the pile. His fourth shot hit the left half on the log, and the timber rolled over the pile onto the men crouched behind it.

There were screams of pain and curses, but no one ran.

"Hope it broke a few bones back there," said Dan.

"Hey Sweets, you still with us or are you hurt too bad?" shouted Dan.

"Don't you worry yourself about me black boy. You're the one who'll be dead by morning."

"That sun getting a little too hot? Your men can use the well to get a drink of water if you want. You know I wouldn't shoot a man just going for water."

"My men are okay. We'll wait a bit and have plenty of food and water out here."

"How about a shovel? You want to bury the dead men before they stink even worse than they do now?"

The answer this time was intense fire for several minutes.

Dan chambered another round in the big gun and fired through the wagon bottom again. No visible results this time.

"Hey Sweets, you think Elva is okay?"

"Of course she's fine. You don't have to worry about her at all."

"I'm just hoping she has a place to go after I kill you. Once I have you all dead, I'm heading off to burn your ranch."

Again intense fire rained onto the cabin.

"Damn Sweets, sometimes I think you got no sense of humor at all."

Watching the wood chunks blown from the cabin wall, he thought, "They keep chipping away and this place will finally fall in."

Many rounds came through the ports during periods of intense fire, but the cabin being higher than where the defenders lay, the bullets flew through the openings and embedded into the walls over the defenders' heads. Luckily no one had been hit.

At heavy twilight, Dan huddled with Jake and Anne for a minute. "I'm going out for a quick look-see. Be back in ten minutes. Get the kids' faces covered with that ash slurry, so they don't stand out in the dark." He pulled the bolts holding the hidey-hole in place and slowly wormed his way out of the opening.

Rising to a crouch, once outside, he could see no one around. He began to crawl slowly around the east side of the building, stopping next to the porch. He could hear the attackers getting restless. It had been a long day for those baking in the sun. The war had begun early in the day, and those who were geared for war felt the need for action stirring their blood. The beast can be hard to hold in check once he has been fed.

One man, bending low, came running up to the porch, deposited a bundle of brush next to the porch and began trying to light it.

Dan sprang at him, clubbing the attacker on the head with his colt pistol. The man fell hard. Remaining close to the ground, Dan used his pistol as a club, breaking fingers in each of the man's hands. The man was lucky, only wounded, he would not die tonight. I'm getting soft, thought Dan, shoulda cut his throat. He wouldn't be firing weapons against them tonight. Dan retreated to the opening and went back into the cabin.

"It's time," said Dan. "They's starting to mill around out there. I can see them scurrying from rabbit hole to rabbit hole."

Water based slurry had darkened all their faces and hands to make them more difficult to see. While they dabbed and wiped it on, Jake removed the log below the rear house port. Dan put the stock of his buffalo gun in the cook stove. Quietly watching the curling flames begin to eat the stock. Damn, he thought, I'm going to miss that gun.

"Jake," said Dan, "lead them straight up the hillside. I'm going to watch the exit for a minute to slow them down. I'll be with you in five minutes or less. We're going over this hill to the valley below, then heading west. I will call to you when I get near."

One attacker stuck his pistol through the front portal and began firing. Dan, standing near the stove, grabbed the wood poker, swung it high, and smashed the man's hand. A scream sounded outside and the pistol dropped to the floor of the cabin.

Jake squeezed his long frame through the portal first, then helped Anne and the children. Dan, still looking out the front port, saw shadows grouping for a rush. He levered a few shots at them, then unfastened the door and ran to the back wall of the cabin, dropping his last box of Sharps ammo into the cook stove. His second time through the opening went faster. Once through the opening, he drew his pistol and waited. He heard them smash into the front door and run into the cabin firing their weapons. Puzzled by the empty room, they searched for the opening. "Here it is," came the cry and soon one cowboy began to work his bulk through the opening. The bullets began to fire in the cook stove. Their rising roar panicked the cowhands who fled the cabin. The attacker still coming through the gun portal tried to pull himself through faster, only to meet Dan's Colt head on. The cold, heavy steel dropped him motionless. The sounds of the exploding ammo were beginning to die out in the cabin, so Dan, leaning over, emptied his pistol through the top of the port, turned, and ran up the hill.

"I'm Dan, I'm Dan," he sang as he ran up the hill. He stopped behind a gnarly old trunk and reloaded his pistol. Turning back to the cabin, he saw the mass of shadows begin to filter around the sides of the building. He emptied his pistols at them, watched the scattered confusion amongst the men, turned and ran before they could reform.

He caught up with his group at the crest of the hill. Jake, leading the way, had Anne by the hand. Loss of blood and the pain of his
wound had slowed his progress, he fought hard to keep up. Picking
up Jewel, Dan began to slowly run down the hill. The descent helped
Jake move faster with Anne under his good arm helping support him.
When they finally splashed through the water of the small rivulet,
the desperate band turned west heading for the cave. The distance
deceiving dark had Dan sure he'd missed it; he stopped to listen.
There was no sound of pursuit. He continued walking west feeling
that if they were unable to find the cave, distance would be their
best ally. A brush growth to his right slowed him. He saw what he
believed could be the cave. Sitting Jewel down, he began searching
the hillside frantically. As panic began to set in, his arm went through
the bushes and he pulled them aside to reveal the rocky entrance.

'Here, here it is," he murmured to the small band as relief surged
through him. He held the brush aside while the party entered. He lit
a match to show Jake and Anne the interior of the cave, quickly dous-
ing the light. He turned to Jake, "How bad is it? If we prop you up
behind the rocks, can you and Anne hold it?"

"Have to," said Jake. "Tighten my bandages to stop the bleeding
and I'll be okay. The kids can stay behind that big boulder while Anne
and I fight them off if they find us."

"I'll be back by first light," said Dan. "I'm going to lead them away
from here. It's time they know what it's like to fight a shadow. A
quick draw and bravado won't be much good out here. By morning,
they'll be back at the Slash S hoping to save it. Take care of Anne and
the kids, Jake. You have our lives in your hands."

"Don't go, Dan, stay here," Anne said.

"I can't, darling. It's not the way I fight." He kissed Anne and ran
out the entrance. "It's time these thugs faced a skilled night fighter.
Time to put fear into their souls."

Turning east down the valley, he ran slowly in the dark, stum-
bling and tripping. He heard the Sweets' riders still coming down the

hillside and he ran into the stream, splashing past them to get their attention.

Lead flew past him, and he turned up the far hill onto solid ground. Stopping behind a tree, he pulled his pistol and waited for the pursuers. Their front man ran past his tree, only to be almost torn into two pieces when Dan fired into his side. At a distance of two feet the .45 caliber round smashed into the gunhand's chest killing him instantly. Dan could hear others falling to the ground for protection, and he ran straight up the hill away from them. The ground was being torn up off to his left side from blind firing by his attackers. He stayed his course, running faster now, filled with hot bullet adrenaline pounding in his chest. He ran uphill until he found a wide game trail, turned to the east and followed it for twenty to thirty yards. He fired his pistol back at the gunhands, revealing his presence, hoping they would follow him. He repeated this maneuver several times until he was sure they were following him. Then with his long lope and years of Indian training, he turned his mind to running and worked hard at eating up the miles to the Slash S.

Light rain began to fall, soon he was soaked, but the wet felt good against his heated body. Hours later with a severe pain in his side, the trail turned downward and he knew the prairie was close. At the far edge of flatness, he stopped, listening behind him. He heard nothing, too late to change his course now. He needed to continue his attack on the Sweets' ranch.

His vulnerability increased once he ran out on the prairie, no cover and a multitude of enemies. Still, now he could pick up the pace and he ran onward toward the only light he could see in the distance, believing it to be the Slash S ranch. He passed cattle that turned to look at him, but they avoided all contact. There must be men out riding herd, but he was able to avoid them completely. A night rider wouldn't be looking for a running man. Dan believed the ranch would now be held by the working cowboys, while the gunhands had ridden with Sweets. He slowed to a walk the last hundred yards, remaining in the shadow of the barn, and avoiding the light thrown wide by the gas lantern hanging in the middle of the yard.

At the corner of the barn, Dan saw one cowboy walking across the yard, carrying a rifle. Obviously he was the night sentry. Holding his knife in his right hand, Dan slowly began to stroll out in the yard in a path that would pass close to the man. The watchman became aware of him. "Who are you?" he challenged Dan.

"The last man you ever wanted to see," said Dan.

The man turned, trying to swing the rifle at Dan, but the blade of the knife entered upward through his chin and into his skull before he could fire the weapon. Lifeless, he dropped straight down and lay motionless. "Shame a man should have to die because of his boss's greed," thought Dan. He entered the barn, lit the lantern hanging by the door, and saddled a bay stalled near the door. As he left the barn, he tossed the lantern into a pile of straw, and rode for the open prairie.

Mounted on a horse that showed a lot of bottom, Dan kicked it into high speed as he dashed back across the prairie, avoiding the cattle and their riders. He reached the foothills rapidly. The pines were small and clustered here. He dismounted and walked the bay through the growth trying to find the game trail he had followed earlier.

A shot broke through the silence of the trees and Dan stopped all motion. Listening hard to the quiet, he was sure a hunter of men was close. The shot had come from his right side. The sound had not passed close to him. He felt safe in the dark, believing the man was panicked and had been hoping for a lucky shot. Shaking his feet from the stirrups, he slid off the bay. Too fine an animal to get hit by a wild bullet. Dan tied him to a lower branch. He stepped forward slowly, Colt in his hand.

Stepping slowly, one long pace at a time, watching, listening, he came upon Sweets lying near a clump of brush.

"Drop your gun," Dan said. "I'll shoot you where you lay, you cursed dog."

"Don't!" cried Sweets, "Don't shoot me alone here. The men are gone and you're in no danger."

The old man threw his weapon away and lay helpless on the ground before Dan. A wound high on his left leg had brought him down.

"Those skunks just dropped me here and ran; a batch of cowards. When they saw the fire, they knew I was finished. Men hired for guns truly have no loyalties."

A flood of anger surged through Dan. The pent up hatred of Sweets had built up strong during the long day's battle. He cocked his pistol and stepped closer to the downed man. Aiming right at the old man's chest, he felt he must rid the earth of the evil represented by the arrogant bastard lying helpless.

Sweets tried to back away, using his arms and one good leg, pushing and clutching at anything for cover. He knew he deserved no mercy coming from Pinkney after his action of the previous day.

"Please don't kill me. You've already won," he begged. His words were so stricken with fear they had little meaning. Dan's finger tightened on the trigger. Sweets' hands were raised to fend off the bullet, but the now heavy Colt barrel slowly lowered to the ground. He returned his gun to its holster. Killing an opponent in a fight was one thing. Murdering a helpless old man, no matter what the cause was something Pinkney could not do.

"It'd be plain out cold blooded slaughter and I just can't do it," he said. "You'd a had no mercy for me. Still I won't do it. Where are you wounded, Candras?"

"It's my leg. You shot me at the wagon, almost killed me, but we got the bleeding to stop."

"Think you can sit a horse?"

"If I can get mounted."

"I'll be back with your horse, and I will assist you, but you better not pull another weapon out or I will kill you," he said as he tied the big bay mount securely near Candras. He helped the wounded man to his feet. Once Sweets got a grip on the pommel and his good leg in the stirrup, Dan was able to push him into the saddle. Handing him the reins, he said, "Just ride toward that light of the burning barn. Don't worry, I only lit the barn, and your good men are still there. They would have protected everything else."

Dan led him to the edge of the prairie and watched him ride off.

"Should a killed that bastard," he thought and turning began to trot back up into the forest, trying to locate the game trail. Legs burning and feeling the exhaustion in his body, hungry as he could ever remember being, the thought of Anne and the kids drove him forward in the dark.

When the sky grudgingly gave up a little light, he found the trail he was searching for and began walking. A long stride ate up miles and stretched his aching thighs. He broke into a run again and soon passed the area where the cabin lay off to the left. He could still smell the smoke, the homestead was certainly burned, but what had been built could be rebuilt, as long as he had Anne by his side. In the growing light he found the cave easily and called to Jake and Anne.

Anne ran out the entrance, stopped short of him, just looking at him. Then she flung herself into his arms, "Dan. Oh Dan, you're back."

"I will always return to you my love. Thanks be to God that you and the children are safe. Bad news, our place has been fired. No sense in hurrying back to a burned out homestead, Anne. We'll rebuild and the country will be better now. Let's go in and look at some vittles."

A large meal and a long sleep brought Dan back to consciousness late that afternoon. He learned from Jake that the attackers never found the cave. The kids had been warm and slept all night. Jake's arm was healing nicely and he was eager to look at the cabin. "Possibly," he thought, "something can be salvaged." They were all sure there would be weeks or maybe months of work ahead, but now it was permanent, forever work that would be for the future.

Loaded up, the small band trudged back with reluctant feet. Their worst fears were realized. Everything had gone under the torch. They began sifting through the ashes, but nothing was salvageable. Several of the horses had returned, and Dan quickly had them enclosed in what was left of the corral, held in by only a rope fence. One of the animals was his trusty mount.

Dan, with Adam's help, began digging graves for the four dead riders. Everyone's spirits were low, when they heard a small bark from the tree line, and a bedraggled looking mutt came racing home.

At full speed, he jumped into Adam's arms almost knocking him over. "Ruff, you made it. Thought those bad men got you." The mud covered dog coated Adam with a fresh layer of Montana dirt, but no one cared. The small band was now complete. Somehow the resilience of the small dog avoiding the attackers, hiding out through the night, and waiting for them to return, raised everyone's mood.

Jake began a campfire. The cook stove in the cabin had been destroyed by the falling roof.

Soon Anne had a pan of cornbread and bacon cooking. The delicious smell and the cooling night air had everyone hungry. Dan brought a bucket of water up from the well, and they ate hungrily. Fortunately the well was okay, they had feared the attackers would dump a dead horse into it to ruin the water. Dan felt they might have been too lazy to drag the horse that far.

During the course of the meal, a wagon was seen approaching. They could make out several men and a woman. Dan and Jake had their weapons ready, but quickly saw they wouldn't be needed. Elva Sweets pulled up and with help stepped off the wagon.

"Don't know if you folks'll accept help from us right now, but I'm here to offer what I can. First, my sincere apology for the barbaric act of my husband. I had no prior knowledge or by God, I swear I'd have been in the cabin with you fighting.

"Candras made it back. Thanks to you Dan. He's still very ill, but I think that tough old coot will make it. He needs a lot of healing in his mind and his body. It was a kindness that you helped him, Mr. Pinkney. We will always be grateful. I swear he's a changed man. He'll be good now. If I have to I will take a switch to him every day.

"Friori and his band are gone. I expect we will never to see them again. They rode off on Slash S mounts. The whole bunch never did enough work to warrant even one horse.

"I brought several men to bury our dead. I see you started, but they can finish it. It's properly our work. Our barn has burned down, which turned out to be a good thing. Without that light to guide him, Candras would have died, lost on the prairie. Our house is in good shape, and you are all welcome to come and stay as long as you would like to."

"Thanks to you, Elva. You have a large heart, but I won't leave my homestead. We'll make our future in the next days with work, then we'll have a cabin. My man, Dan, will see to it."

"I understand honey, truly I do, iffin you don't mind, I'll leave these two hands to get some of the logs cut today."

"That'd be a great help, Elva. Jake's bad arm leaves the sawing all to Dan."

Elva called to her men. "Sam, Slim, come here for a minute." She handed them a basket of food, blankets, saws and axes. "You're staying here tonight. When you finish the graves, I want you to help Mr. Pinkney fell a few logs. Just do as he directs. I'll be back in the morning with more men and some horses. So Dan, you might want to work on that corral first. Use that wire Candras brought for you. That'll speed everything up.

"Anything else you think you might need?" she asked.

"Thank you for being neighborly," said Anne. "Hope Candras is feeling better. We should be just fine now."

It was a long night with little bedding, the family and Jake huddled close together for warmth. A merry fire kept everyone's spirits up and after hot coffee with breakfast, Dan and the cowboys walked up the hill to drop a few trees. Straight and tall was what they were looking for. They cut fast and let the logs lie until Elva would return with the horses. Near high sun, Elva rode in with a wagon and four more men. Behind her rode another dozen townsmen, who having heard of the fire came to help erect a new place for the family to live in.

Anne picked a spot twenty yards to the east so they would remain close to the well. Jake's cabin was to be built close to where the first building was. The corral went up fast for the new horses. Then the serious work began. By heavy twilight, the Pinkney house was up and habitable.

Elva brought her wagon up to the new cabin and pulled down the tarp she had in the back of her wagon revealing a new cook stove for Anne.

"Elva, you're a treasure," said Anne running over to hug the woman. "Thank you so much."

"Just part of being a good neighbor," said Elva as she and her men drove away.

Dry Creek Feast

AS PINK AND yellow streaks chased the dark further west, Anne, Dan, and the family hitched the wagon up and were headed to the Sweets' ranch. Jake wanted a day of rest and was sitting quietly smoking a homemade as the horses began their work for the day. Several hours of easy riding had them pulling into the Sweets' yard.

Standing quietly at her door, Elva descended the veranda steps and welcomed them inside. "So nice of you to bring Adam and Jewel," she told Anne. "Come on kids, make yourselves at home in my place."

Dan brought up the tail end of the group. "Suppose I better talk to Candras," he said, and Elva took him upstairs to where the old looking man lie quietly, following Dan with only his eyes. His white face showed no emotion, and he looked at Pinkney as a fighter who has just been totally defeated.

"What do you want?" he asked in a low voice.

"Mostly, I want total cessation of all hostilities, now and going into the future."

"No worry there. Fiori and his band of renegades rode north two days ago. I can't believe how he turned my head. There is nothing I can say about the attack. I was wrong, felt too pushed at the time, but still totally wrong."

"Let's not talk about that day ever again," said Dan. "The truth as I see it is that this valley needs you. You are a vital force. No one knows what went down at the homestead except us, and I suggest we leave it at that."

"I'll readily agree to that. They would drive me from the valley if they knew. Elva and I are too old to begin again, seems very generous of you."

"One more thing," said Dan, "I plan on putting up that fence, and our former agreement for open water stands with me."

"Accepted with gratitude." Candras raised himself in his bed, no longer a fire breather, he seemed a small dried husk of a man, but he held his hand out to Dan.

As they shook, Candras said, "You can trust me all the way, Pinkney. I can see that you are a man of honor, and I will try to live up to your example."

After tea and cakes with Elva, they took the now friendly road into Dry Creek. Anne needed utensils, dishes, and supplies. Dan wasn't sure how far his limited money would go, but maybe now they could swing an I. O. U. with the grim faced general store man.

They took their rig to the livery and strolled to the store. Dan heard his name called, turned to see Dave Vegas. "Harve is sitting in the bar. He's been shot bad and asking to speak with you. Better hurry, not sure how long he can hold on."

Dan started for the bar, but heard Dave call him again. He had his hand stuck out, "Sorry about what I done before. Welcome to our community. Can we let our bygones be forgotten?"

Dan shook his hand. "We stepping out on new ground from now on, Dave."

Harve was slumped in a chair, his shirt crimson with fresh blood. "Fiori shot me. He's got a bad hate for you. I tried to leave the bunch and he gut-shot me, still angry that I lost that fight with you. Said everything was laid on my head."

"It was a fair fight between you and me. I didn't have no hard feelings," said Dan. "I made peace with Sweets today."

"That's gentle of you. No hard feelings eases me. Watch out for Fiori, cause Sweets was never a part of it. Fiori had him so twisted with greed. The old man never stood a chance. Most of what we was doing was Fiori," he said as his eyes moved to a blank stare as he passed.

If Sweets had been right, Fiori had ridden north with his gang of pistoleros. He should be far way by now. What would cause him to return here? Still, the fresh blood on Harve certainly spoke that he was close. No man could have traveled far with that wound. Dan's mind was racing with the bad possibility that an evil gun still lurked near Dry Creek.

He walked back to the store to see how Anne was fairing with her shopping. Perplexed with the problem, he was not as alert as he usually was. Sweets' power had been broken, Fiori's men had been thoroughly beaten and would not have returned here where they were known. Men had died for a lost cause. Why come back except to face more death. Gunhands were interested in money, not revenge.

As he waked past the livery stable, he called out to Anne. She might have finished at the store and returned for the wagon.

Twilight was slowly dropping the light level. They should return to the cabin soon. He was sure the kids were tired and ready to sleep. Maybe Anne could fix up a comfortable place in the wagon for them on the long ride home.

The wrong voice answered him from the stable. A deep chill shot through his body.

"Figured I would run, didn't you? Well you're right in a way, as soon as your carcass is lying there bleeding on the street, I'll ride out. You're right to stop right there though, I have my gun aimed right at you. I'm going to shoot you low, let you suffer a long time."

"Fiori?"

Sweat rolled down Dan's forehead, stinging his eyes. His body singing with tension, he sought a way out.

"Not really sure you can beat me to the draw are you, Al? That's as I figured, thought you's a coward from the start."

"You probably right. Been around a lot of brave dead men. I've never been a fool, Pinkney. I knew you were fast, first time I saw you. In another minute, you'll be dead and I'll be riding out of here. Ain't no one going to be sitting around wondering who was the fastest. No other man in town's got the sand to challenge me."

Trying to locate Fiori from the sound of his voice and recalling the inside of the livery, The Kid knew the area was too big to hit Fiori with one shot. It would be playing a deadly hand of bad roulette at best.

"Dan," he heard Anne call him. Hoping that his adversary had looked at the sound, he leaped to his left, drawing both Colts at the same time. He began throwing lead through the open door into the dark. He was vaguely aware that bullets were flying past him, but he was absorbed in trying to fire at the flashes he saw in the stable.

Suddenly men were running from the street and gathered around him. A lantern now lit in the building cast a flickering light on the dead body of the outlaw. A grim hole had been punched through the man's face and blood was leaking onto his sun darkened skin.

MacCaffee was on the street next to him, and knowing the draining emotions and weakness after a gun fight, helped Dan to his feet. "You've done it, Mr. Pinkney. You've rid the town of the last evil."

Townsmen gathered around him, saying words of gratitude, but Dan elbowed his way through the crowd with halting muscles searching for Anne. She ran to his arms.

"Will it never end?" she asked him.

"It's done now, lets us head home.

Made in the USA
Charleston, SC
02 April 2016